"AIMLESS TRIGGERS" BULLETS AIN'T GOT A NAME

JOSE HERNANDEZ JR.

Aimless Triggers: Bullets Ain't Got A Name

By

Jose C. Hernandez Jr.

Cadmus Publishing
CadmusPublishing.com

Aimless Triggers: Bullets Ain't Got A Name

Web: Cadmuspublishing.com

Facebook.com/Cadmuspublishing

Business email: admin@cadmuspublishing.com

ISBN# 978-1-63751-538-9

Library of Congress Control Number 9781637515389

Book Catalog Info Categories:

Urban/Hood Novel

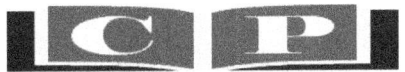

Cadmus Publishing

CadmusPublishing.com

Introduction:

It always starts off the same way, it never fails. Maybe in different types of ways or for different types of reasons, but nine times out of ten, it's all senseless. Trouble usually starts over a piece of pussy, or you going to the corner store and catch a dude giving you a sideways look just cause of a certain type of color hanging out of your back pocket. It's all circumstances of you being at the wrong place at the wrong time, but what if that's not the case? What if God intended for you to be at that exact place at that exact time just so you can become some type of ripple effect for somebody else's life? Who really knows other than God, right? I can't answer that mysterious question for you but one thing life has taught me and from personal experience is that if you try to live righteously and be a good person to society shit seems to go south for you no matter how hard you try to do right. But live on the edge and have no care for anybody, or the world, shit just falls into place. Ironic ain't it? My story isn't like any other "hood story', some are going to try to dispute that. All I can say is " hate on hater, this this is my story so of course it's not like any other hood story. It ain't easy being young, handsome and brown in my hood ya feel me playa? So kick back, relax and puff, puff, pass while you ride shotgun with me holding the wheel.

"Here We Go"
By: Z-Ro

Chapter 1

2002 Mid July (Wednesday)

(Book One)

My lungs felt like they were going to burst with all the heavy breathing I was doing. I wasn't sure what was going to happen, but what I did know was I had to get some where and fast! I cut corners hard, thank God for Michael Jordan coming thru for me right now cause my kicks were sure gripping that concrete. Who knew that Nike was making shoes to save lives in the street as well and not just for basketball. I was determined to make it home, I jumped fences or whatever got in front of me. I went over it, thru it, whatever it took for me to stay ahead of the two clowns chasing me trying to punch my time clock and I wasn't trying to check out just yet. If God says it's time to go, it's time to go and I get that, but I wasn't trying to hear it. I was on a mission and that was to keep living. I finally catch a break and see a car pulling up to a gate to some apartments ahead of me and it's waiting for the gate to fully open and I head that way. Me and the car both go thru the gate at the same time and the gate immediately starts to close as soon as the car and I go thru.

Thank God. Safe! I heard a big crash behind me and turn to look and see that my buddies didn't make it and I stop instantly and turn around.

"Ha Ha ! Bitch ass niggas, ya'll thought ya'll had me!" I scream to the two dudes on the other side of the gate.

"Fuck you! We gonna catch yo bitch ass when we see you again. Come to the Spice again and see what happens! Oh crab ass nigga!" One of the two yell at me.

"Crips rule all Bloods"! I yell back.

"C's up B's down". I continue to holler while I use my hand to gesture the letter c and b alphabets and turn around in one smooth motion and continue to run off. I was safe right now and luck was on my side and I wasn't trying to test it at all.

I reached into the pocket of my sweaty starched down jeans and pull out my bent soggy blunt and Bic blue lighter and lean up against a wall of the apartments to catch my breath. I still had about half a mile to go before I finally make it to my neighborhood in Alief. I put my lighter to my blunt and run the flame on it and try to dry it up as best as possible. I hear the blunt sizzle and I can smell the aroma of the chocolate flavor Philly blunt paper and finally focus the flame to one side of the blunt. I let it get cherry red before I finally put the blunt to my lips and take a deep puff. I felt a sensation of relief instantly as the smoke passed thru my lungs and started coughing right after inhaling. "Damn, that's some fire" I thought to myself. I pull on the blunt a couple more times and catch my balance and push off the wall and start walking home again with all the calm in the world. I totally forgot about running for my life and now here I am like nothing ever happened. Crazy, right?

I finally get to the entrance to my neighborhood and see the big stone plaque in the middle of the two way street that reads "Welcome To Imperial Point" Where I lived wasn't a "ghetto" per sé, but it was hood as hell. At some point it was full of white, middle class people, you know, that shit you see on t.v. But then the Mexicans and blacks started getting a little bit of money and we moved in. That sure got the white folks out the way, fast. I ain't racist, hell I'm Latino and bang CRIP, but I'm just telling you how it is. Houston was growing and people just had to live somewhere nice, so why not go where all the nice houses are, right?

I finally make it to the house and get inside and couldn't wait to get out of my jeans, damn Sta-Flo ain't made to last after running for a few blocks in this Texas weather.

"Mom! Mom, you home?" I call out for momma. Her van's out front, but no one's home. Oh well.

I go to my room and empty my pockets before taking my pants off. Keys, pocket knife, money clip with the letter C on it, complements of my Dad, and finally my sack of bud. What we will do to get some weed. I hate going to Spice Ln. to score, but Roc gots the best weed around and if I need a sack then I'm gonna get my sack from him. Plus, it's good to see his baby momma too, especially after what happened between me and Peaches. I remember it like it was just yesterday.

4 Months Ago

I was running low on some bud and had to re-up and I mean a/sap! So I called my "killa man" up. It's what we call our weed man around here so the laws don't know what we talking about. You say "my dope man" or some shit like that we know you ain't from around here. It was code for us and if you from where I'm from you know what I'm talking about. Phone ringing, no answer.

"Fuck it, I'ma just pull up" I said to myself. Half the time he was around anyways. I got ready and shot that way.

(Knock, Knock)

"Hey Cris, what's going on Bay-be?" said Peaches when she opened the door for me and when I tell you she looked so fine I ain't even exaggerating. She was short, like 5' tall, not too dark and not too light. Real hair and a real fat booty with some good size titties. They ain't made like that anymore, all these hoes now a days got injections and shit. Not Peaches, all natural thick and pretty as fuck.

"Wassup ma, Roc around?" I asked. My eyes were shaded with my Loc's on my face. It was a good thing too, cause I was eye balling every bit of her. She knew it too.

"He ain't here" she responded with that sexy New Orleans accent, at least hurricane Katrina helped H-town out a bit by bringing us

some fine ass Cajun women to grace our city. "Damn" I said, sounding all bummed out and leaning up against the door frame.

"I need some killa bad! You got some to sell me?" I asked her

"Naw, I only got my personal shit! She told me and she shifted her wait

I finally noticed that she was bare foot and her toes were painted light green and they looks so sexy and ready to be sucked on one by one.

"I got a blunt rolled up and I was just fince to smoke it. I'll smoke with you, Roc isn't going to be around for a minute and I know how it is to be out. Come in, "She told me stepping aside to let me in.

Oh did I forget to mention that she stripped?

I stepped inside with no hesitation and she closed the door behind me. It was ice cold and it smelled of bud and candles, a lil messy with fast food bag's and big gulps sitting around, but for the most part the place was clean.

"Sit down boy, you're scared of me or something?" She said. I wanted to say "yes."

"Nah ma." I said brushing her comment off and sat on the love seat. She sat Right next to me.

"Oh shit." I thought to myself.

I take my shades off and start to relax. A remote control appears in her hand out of nowhere and the stereo starts bumbing, Jodeci is doing their best shit. She looks at me with some cat eyes and all I could do is smirk. She does too.

"You smell good Cris, what cologne is that?" She asked and she actually leaned in closer to me.

"Uhm, It's called Burberry London". I say to her..

"Mmm, I like it. I might get it for Roc but it all depends," she said

"Depends on what?" I asked.

She just smirked at me.

She reached over to the coffee table and picked up a fat ass blunt, a ball bat is what we call them around here. She put her lighter to it and I could instantly smell the strawberry flavor of the cigar she used to roll her weed in. It got cherry red and then put the blunt to her lips and took a deep ass pull of the blunt. She didn't even cough!

She then passes it to me. I guess she think I'm nervous when I grab it from her cause she then puts a hand on my knee and tells me,

"Relax bay be." She purrs and exhales a big cloud of smoke. I take some good hits and I finally cough.

It made her laughs at me and I hit it again and again.

"You gonna let me hit it or are you going to baby sit my shit?"

She asks teasingly but serious.

"My bad, damn," that's some fire: I say in between coughs.

"I know, right" she says taking a hit and looking at me some type of way

"How old are you Cris?" She asked me before taking another hit. Smoke crept off the blunt and it traced her eye and she squinted, but it made her look sexy as hell.

"I'm fince to be 16 in September". I said and she passed me the blunt as her jaw dropped.

"Oh my God, you're still a bay-be" she cooed.

"Yeah," I say with a little laugh."

"You're really cute, you act a little older tho. It's probably cause you fucking all these lil hoochies around here huh?" She says with a big smile on her face.

"Nah, not really". I was tripping, she wasn't flirting was she?

"Liar! I bet you got about 10 girls and fucking all the time. Don't lie," she tells me.

"I'm still a virgin." Woah! I know I didn't just tell this fine ass lady that shit. Fucking weed.

"Oh my God! Forealz?!" she say's excited.

Fuck it the cat's out of the bag.

"I mean, I've got my dick sucked and I've ate some pussy but that's it." I confess to her.

She sits back on her couch, blows smoke out, and crosses her thick juicy legs all at the same time and just looks at me like she was searching my face to see if I was lying. I was a little embarrassed so I just stayed quiet.

"So tell me, what exactly have you done to a girl?" She asks me.

"Well, uhm". I clear my throat.

"I've ate pussy, sucked titties, fingered them." I say

"But never actually stuck your dick in a girl before?" She asks with astonishment and licks her lips.

7

"No." I say to her and feel ashamed like I did something I had no business without actually doing it.

I don't know if it was the weed or what, but her eyes got super glassy all of a sudden.

"So you think you know how to please a woman?" She asked me in a sexy voice that made my dick a little chubby.

All of a sudden she stands up and at the same time "Freakin You" by Jodeci comes on the stereo.

Peaches is standing right in front of me and she hooks her thumb into the waist line of her little boy shorts and drops them. This girl didn't even have any panties on and her pussy was so clean shaven and so fucking pretty. My heart was beating so fast. Next her spaghetti tube top is popped over her head and guess what? No fucking bra! Can you believe it? Them things didn't have any support at all! Damn, they gotta be fake.

She straddles me hard, basically jumps on me and we start kissing and my hands instantly grab her ass cheeks. She had a big ass and it was so soft and then she grabs one of her titties and pops it in my mouth. They had to be real.

"Eshhh" she sucks in air thru her teeth and moans while I suck on her nipple. She grinds on top of me and my dick is super hard.

"Mmm. Damn it." she says and gets off of me and lays on the sofa and opens her legs. All I see is a pretty pink pussy, bald and shiny.

"Show me what you can do Cris." She tells me while she rubs on her clit.

I didn't hesitate for shit and did as I was told and ate away.
"Ooooh bay-be! Mmm. Shit. Eshhh." She crooned in a sexy
voice.

I put my mouth all over that pussy and even stuck a finger in it. I
seen a dude do it to a chick on a porno, so I did it to Peaches.
"Oh shit, Uh, mmm, Oh yeah bay-be. Mmm, eat that pussy." I
start mowing her shit down, and start finger fucking her even faster and
all you could hear was her moaning and the wet sound her pussy was
making with my mouth and finger in it. My face was wet with her pussy
juice and she tasted good, I couldn't believe I was doing this, I mean how
many kids my age were doing this? Most were outside or inside playing
video games, yet here I was with my face in some pussy. Crazy.
"Get up," she tells me and pushes my face out of her pussy.
"Did I do something wrong?" I asked confused.
"Let's see what else you can do bay-be" she says. She grabs my
hands and pulls me to her bedroom. She grabs me and pushes me on her
bed and she starts to undo my jeans. She pulls my jeans down only so far.
Damn starch.
"Hold up ma" I say trying to get out of my pants. Fuck my
crease! I ain't get out of my pants completely when she drops my boxers
and pops my dick in her mouth and I fall on her bed.
"Oh shit damn mami! Shit! God! I say while she sucks my dick
hard.*
I don't know what got into me but all of a sudden I blurted out
some crazy shit.

9

"I love you baby," I said and she busted out laughing.

"Not yet, but you will after this." she says and gets off her knees and walks over to her nightstand.

I couldn't get my eyes off her ass as she walks away. She opened the drawer and got a condom out of it and turned around and looked at me.

"You shouldn't have any problem fitting into this papi" she said and tossed me the pack.

Trojan XL Hmmm I guess.

She walked back over to me and gave me a hand with it. Literally.

"Damn Cris, you sure surprised me daddy. You sure you a virgin or did you just say that so you could fuck me? she asked.

"I am ma, I ain't lying to you." I told her.

"Well after today you won't have to ever lie," she said. She finished rolling the condom on and pushed me on my back, and I crawled backwards onto the bed. I made her come get it. She crawled on top of me and threw her legs on each of my sides. She grabbed my dick and guided my shit into her. It felt so fucking good. We both moaned at the same time and she sat on my dick. She was so hot and juicy I couldn't believe it. I grabbed her ass cheeks and spread them and she grinded on top of me slowly. She leaned over me and we kissed and then I grabbed a tittie and sucked on it.

"Ummm, bay-be, suck them titties Mmm," she moaned and started moving on top of me faster. I brought my knees up and started

pounding hard. "Ah,ah,ah!" she started screaming and my balls were smashing her asshole . "Mm,Mm,Mm! Oh shit. Mm Fuck bay-be!" she moaned louder and louder.

"Damn mami, that pussy feels so good." I said huffing and puffing.

"Fuck this pussy daddy! Fuck me hard. Mmm," she cried and I fucked away.

"Who's pussy is it mami?" I asked.

"It's yours bay-be" she moaned and by her saying that I did it for me.

"I'm coming!" I said pounding hard.

"I'm coming too papi. Ah!,Ah!,Ah!,I'm coming" she screamed and I fucked her harder. After I nutted all up in the condom we lay there with her on top of me and us kissing.

I couldn't believe what just happened, I mean I'm only 16 and here I was ass naked with a sexy fine ass woman at least 10 years older than me. I know kids my age were fucking, but I bet you anything they doing things within their age group.

My thoughts were interrupted by the sound of Peaches, laughing, "Ha,Ha,Ha,He,He." Peaches was laughing not even 5 inches from my face and I looked at with wrinkled eye brows. "Did I do something wrong?" I thought to myself.

"What? What's so funny?" I asked, I couldn't hold a smile back myself.

"I popped your cherry baby, that's what." She told me then planted them juicy lips on mine.

"How was it papi?" She asked me and moved her hips on top of me with me still in her. It started to feel chilly down there.

"Great, it was really great. Best day of my life." I said clearing my throat. She kisses me one more time and pushes herself off of me to get up.

"Not bad for your first time Cris, you got something good right there and I bet you are going to make a girl or some girls very happy." She says and licks her lips and stares at me as I lay there butt naked and hanging sideways.

"You think so ma, for real?" I liked how she was giving me props and stroking my ego.

"Yeah, you'll have the ladies coming back for you. Just don't be an asshole Cris. Just cause a girl is a hoe or whatever always treat them with respect and like a lady. That's very important to us." She told me with a very serious look on her face.

I know now that she was giving me some real good game that I was going to put to use for the rest of my life. Thank you Peaches. I left Peaches' apartment a new man. Chest out, shoulders square and ready to take on the world with the smell of pussy on my face and a pocket full of weed.

"Tear it up"
By: Young Jeezy

Chapter 2

Present

I took a shower cause I hate being sweaty and I won't dare lay in my bed dirty. My mom always kept the crib clean and she hated a messy house. Me and my sister Lorena took up after our mom and became neat freaks ourselves. It was just us three Lorena was 5 years younger than me and we've been living in the same house for seven years, right after my mom and dad separated. My dad was around, but he lived with his now current wife Raquel and their 4 year old daughter, my sister Julie. Raquel was working at a car dealership and my dad was the manager, that's how they met. He was the best salesman and making good money, we ain't hurt for nothing, my mom either. But shit happens and my mom found out that my dad was having an affair and filed for divorce. Now my pop's has his own car lot and Raquel is his only receptionist, guess she isn't going to give another chick a chance at my dad like she had.

I got dressed and turned my computer on that I got for Christmas to play some jams that I also use it to burn CD's. It's a lil side hustle, ya feel me? And it really comes in handy when I go to house parties and pop in a CD with the latest jams that ain't even out yet and it's good for business. One for ten or two for fifteen, just like the dopeman. I had just put some Bone Thugs on and started grinding some weed up to roll up and blaze before my mom and Lorena got back from wherever they went. My mom ain't trip about smoking, just not in the crib. After she caught me high she sat me down and told me it was o.k. and that she prefer me to smoke at home and be safe than to be running the streets and risk getting locked up. She also admitted she put too much pressure on my pop's with all her rules and it's probably why he stepped out of their marriage and didn't want to lose the next most important man in her life which was me.

I had just put the last bit of saliva on my ball bat when my cordless started crying. I answered without even looking at my caller ID.

"Yo, wassup?" I said after I put the phone between my neck and shoulder and not losing focus on the mission at hand. Literally.

"Hey handsome, where you been papi?" Asked my current girl, Reneé , with her sexy voice of a whisper.

"Just got back from re-upping babe, wassup with you mami?" I asked.

"Nothing, been calling all morning. Now ya see why you need to get a cell?" She scolded me.

"For what? So you can keep track of me all the time?" I said and laughed.

"Babe, did you go to Roc's at Spice Ln." She asked, worried and upset.

"Yeah, duh, where, where else would I go?" I said back.

"Cris, you know you can't be going over there like that, they'll kill you, then what will I do?" she said to me.

"Find another nigga and move on." I told her joking.

"Fuck you Cris! Stop playing babe." she said seriously.

"I'm just playing baby. Chill, ain't nobody gonna replace me." I told her.

Me and Reneé first met in the ninth grade and had a few common friends but we really didn't meet each other until we was at a skipping party and we hit it off quick. She wasn't like all the other girls around, it was like she was in college or something with the way she carried herself. She was Mexican and didn't speak a lick of Spanish, hence why I called her coconut. Brown on the outside white on the inside.

We had been friends for a few months and always talked on the phone late nights. Then one day at a skipping party things got crazy. We was all high as a kite and I caught Reneé looking at me serious as hell across the room while everybody else was laughing at my homeboy Coy, acting stupid. I was cracking up when all of a sudden Reneé gets up and walks to me and grabs me by the hand and pulls me up. The room got super quiet and everybody looked at us while she drug me to the next room and closed the door behind us. I had no idea she was that strong and didn't know what the fuck was going on? It crossed my mind that I was about to get some. After Peaches it was like girls automatically knew I wasn't a virgin anymore and whenever I went out to a house party, quinceñera , the mall or whatever, I ended up pulling a chick and fucking that night or the next time we met up. Reneé puts her hands on my chest and pushes me up against the door hard. (Bam)!

"Damn Reneé , what the fuck ma?" I asked her serious.

"Give me your phone Cris." She demanded.

"Give you my phone? Girl, if you needed to use my phone you could've just asked. You ain't had to put your hands on a playa like that." I told her and reached in my pocket and handed it to her.

"I don't want to use your phone boy, you are." She told me and started to scroll through my contacts.

"Me, what ya mean?" I asked confused.

"I'm going to give you one chance and one chance only Cris, I want you to call the chick or hoes, whatever you want to call them and tell them that it's over. Do it right here, right now and if you do that me and you can be together," She told me, and she was dead ass serious.

I just looked deep into her eyes and knew I had a once in a lifetime opportunity. We talked about all types of things and the topic of how things would be if we got together came up from time to time. And I always enjoyed those convos between us, shit sounded real good.

I grabbed my phone and made the smart choice and proceeded to carry out my task. She didn't seem too happy that I had to make an extraordinary amount of phone calls. I almost thought that she was going to call the whole thing off, but she stuck it out. Ten minutes later we was kissing passionately and eating each others face off. Plus a broken cell phone as well. That's how we got together.

"You coming over tonight baby?" Asked Reneé on the phone while I walked outside and sparked my blunt up and smoke.

"Yeah babe, I'll be there around 7, k?" I said.

"OK papi, I'll see you then, and save me some of that, I can hear you smoking over there." She giggled.

"Aight baby, I'll see you later. Te' amo mami." I told her.

"Te' amo too papi." She said in her own way in Spanish.

Oh, and Cris." she said off guard to me.

"Wassup babe." I asked puffing away.

"Bring some condoms." She whispered, and I started choking, and not cause of the blunt.

"What?" I asked trying to catch my breath.

"Bay, you know you heard me, you know I hate repeating myself." She told me and hung up.

All I heard was the dial tone and I looked at the phone, clicked the on/off button and could only say one word. "Shit." Me and Reneé have not had sex yet. And that was tough on me. "

"Daddy I'm in love with a gangster"

By Knight Owl.

Chapter 3

I smoked my blunt and reached under my mattress and brought out my .38 special metallic blue snub nose pistol. It was my baby. I loved it like crazy and worshipped it like a god. I carried it with me everywhere and I'm not going to lie though, sometimes I would forget to pack it with me. The crazy thing with that is that when I don't have it on me some bullshit happens. Crazy right? Like today, I rushed out and forgot it and what happens? Two motherfuckers want to test my gangster. I'm real good with my hands, ain't lost a fight since fourth grade. After that, I swore to myself, never again. Reneé hated it cause she felt like I cherished it more than her, but I think she was jealous cause my pistol got oiled and fingered more than she did. But who's fault was that? Not mine. But she understood my lifestyle and respected it as well.

I still haven't had to put a body on it yet, thank God. And I wasn't the one to just bust for no reason. I had morals and if I had to be forced to use it then I had to. I had a few homies who had itchy fingers and would peel your wig back in an instant, no hesitation. Me personally, I'll give you action with your fists and that's why I had unwanted enemies. My mom hated that I could fight , but my dad on the other hand couldn't hide how proud it made him feel. One day he had to go to my school when I was in the 7th grade cause I got into a fight. I thought I was a dead man when I saw my pops turn the corner in the receptionist office. My heart had to stop cause I felt cold instantly when he looked at me.

"And you are?" Asked the lady behind the big desk.

"I'm Cris's father, what's going on?" Asked my dad.

"Please, the principal is waiting for you. You may go in." She said. My dad gave me one last look and we both went in. Shit.

"You should've seen him Anna, the boy can fight!" Exclaimed my dad when he was talking to my mom about his visit to my school.

"I don't give a damn if he can fight Joe! I don't need him always getting suspended for fighting. I have to deal with him all the time, not you!" my mom said. She was pissed.

"Anna, we should put him in boxing." Pleaded my dad.

"Boxing? Are you crazy Joe?! For what? So he can end up all beat up?" Protested my mom.

"Beat up? Him? No Anna, I'm telling you, the boy is good." My dad said.

"And how can you be so damn sure? Only cause he don't got a black eye or busted lip?" Exclaimed my mom. Geez thanks mom.

"I saw it Anna." My dad said proudly.

"You saw what Joe?" Now my mom crossed her arms.

"I saw the video of the fight. Mijo gots a mean left hook!" He said with joy. They never expect that left.

My mom scoffs and starts pacing back and forth. Damn, not good.

She finally stops and faces my dad then cuts her eyes at me then looks at my dad and sees a smirk on his face, and to be honest I think that's the reason why her decision was made.

"No" She said cut and dry.

"But An" My dad barely got those words out.

"I said no! Que no entiendes? No is no in English and Spanish!" Ew, that was cold mom.

My father's shoulders dropped and it looked like he suddenly got deflated cause all the air in him came out in a blast out of his mouth. Defeat.

My mom had fire in her eyes while she looked at him then she looked at me.

"Yo mé encargo de ti despues" She said in Spanish and walked away to her room. (Slam!)

My dad sat down finally on the sofa and just dropped his head.

"I tried mijo, I really would prefer you put your gift to good use. Hopefully it would have kept you out of trouble. Fighting isn't always the right answer son, there are better ways to solve issues. I just want what's best for you and your sister and I need you to be the man of the house. Your mom and your sister both need you here. If something happens to you what do you think will happen to them without you?" He told me, then he finally looks up at me.

"I'm proud of you gordo. Keep that left close eh, they'll be surprised." He said and that smirk appeared again. So did mine.

"Da Youngsta" By:PSK-13

Chapter 4

After I hung up with Reneé I went to my closet and tried to decide what I was going to wear for tonight's occasion. It was going to be a special night for me and Reneé and boy was I ready. I got my best gear out from my choice of cologne (Burberry-Classic) to my drawers (Ralph Lauren), all the way. Purple tag was the way to go, thanks to my pops. I got his taste and money.

I ironed my blue jeans and loaded it down with some Sta-Flo, razor crease. Know what I'm saying?

I shit, shower and shaved and got dressed. I had a skip to my step and felt all giddy like a lil kid.

"Gonna get some pussy, gonna get some pussy...." I kept saying to myself. Thank God for women, gotta love 'em.

I made a slow jam mix CD for tonight. All NB Ridaz on a 90 minute disk. That was enough time right? I hope I can last about 3 songs.

I got dressed and headed to the garage and turned on the light. There she was, all chromed out with the spokes shining and glistening. Nobody could get too close to me while I was swangin in this bad girl or you would lose a leg or something.

The blue pin stripe was awesome on it. It was the cleanest in the whole entire hood and niggas was jealous when I came thru. I popped a CD in my CD player and picked a track. I grabbed my bicycle by the freestyle handlebar, then threw one creased leg over the seat and hit the button to the remote attached to my bike and shot out when it was half way up. It was mid October and it started to get chilly. Only reason why I had starched jeans on. SPM was biting them bars and doing his best shit.

"The room's kinda foggy."

"Ballin is a hobby."

She said "I like your style."

"I told her 'it was doggy'"

"More champagne and more white wine"

"She had a gold chain that looked just like mine"

"Now you may find this a lil hard to believe"

"V.I.P."

By SPM

Chapter 5

I usually go to the corner store a few blocks from my crib, but since I was going to Reneé 's I had to go to another store the opposite direction. Even better 'cause this corner store was off the hook. It was ran by some Arabs and if they knew you well enough and was sure you wasn't a cop or snitch, they let you make it on buying some cigs or brew. Even if you was underage. The way I saw it on why they don't give a fuck about supplying us minors with illegal products was cause they had kids my age or even younger walking around with AK-47's bigger than themselves where they're from. That was just my opinion if you asked me.

As I was pulling up to the store I saw my boy big Ro's black SUV Infinity parked up front and as soon as I got to the curb big Ro was walking out the store, brown baggie in hand.

"Sup Ro, what's cracking cuzz?!" I hollered at Ro.

"Yo Loc's what's good fam?" He called me by my street name. I stayed with a pair of Loc's sunglasses day and night hence the nickname. We shook hands and bumped shoulders. It was a gesture that expressed love in the street with the people you really fucked with and it wasn't for just anybody. You had to earn that respect.

"Where you going cuzz?" Asked Ro.

"Reneé 's. Fince to chill with baby, and you?" I told Ro with a grin.

23

"Just came to get some Phillies and go see my bitch Cookie." Ro said.

Cookie was a white girl that Ro been fucking with ever since I can remember. I ain't going to lie tho, Cookie was a down ass white girl and she would do anything for Ro. Shit if Ro was doing bad and needed some bread Cookie didn't hesitate to meet up with a couple of dudes and let 'em fuck for $200 a pop. I would've fucked too, if she wasn't Ro's chick to be honest. I've known Ro since the sandbox, he was my ace and I didn't have many of them and that's that I got a gang of niggas that got my back. To me, you only got two types of dudes you hang with, and that's your friends and your homeboys. Big Ro was an actual friend, a real true friend. There is a difference. Homies are bound to ride with you and have your back based on rules and regulations, but friends did all that cause it was in their heart and not cause of the same color of bandanas you wore. Plus not just anybody can walk up in your crib without knocking and help himself to a tall cold glass of Kool-Aid.

"Yo Ro, let me run inside and get some shit real quick." I said to Ro.

"Go ahead bro, I'll watch your sister's bike for you." He said and laughed.

"Bitch my shit cleaner than ya momma's ride." I said walking away.

"Cuzz, why you gotta bring my mom's into this?" He said all booty hurt.

"Ha, ha, hol' up cuzz." I went inside and straight to the back where the brew was and got me a 36oz. MD/20-20 the blue one. It ain't a 40oz. but it's gonna do what it do for me.

I went back to the counter and clapped hands with the Arab, dude was real cool. "Buddy, what's going on? Anything else?" He asked with a big ass smile.

"Chillin' let me get a box of honey cigarillos, a box of Marlborough milds and a box of condoms, please." I said, placing my order.

"Ohhh, somebody's getting lucky tonight eh?" His smile got bigger. I couldn't hold my own back.

"Yeah, aye not these bro. Give me the extra lube and extra ribbed." I said matter of factly.

"Ah you know what you doing my friend. Good choice." He rang me up and I paid the man.

"Preciate it." I said grabbing my little brown bag and drink as well and turned to go. As soon as I stepped out I felt the vibe was different instantly and looked at Ro standing still and just staring off into the distance at the street. Like a guard dog.

"Wassup cuzz?" I said and tensed up.

"I just saw them Leawood niggas pass by mean mugging my shit."

Leawood is another neighborhood in Alief. Alief is a big part of the southwest part of Houston big and small at the same time. Especially when you had beef with somebody, you seem to bump into each other all the time. We've been beefing with each other ever since I can remember, and if I recall correctly it was all over some bitch. It's always behind some pussy.

"Fuck them niggas cuzz they ain't talking about shit. I whooped that foo' Guero and dropped his bitch ass at that house party. Remember?" I told Ro.

"Hell yeah! Ha,Ha," Ro responded.

"Plus, you know I stay ready." I said lifting my shirt and letting the pistol grip show a little.

"Shit nigga, you too?" Said Ro and doing the same with his glock.

"Bitch you still can't hit shit even with 16 shots." I said, and laughed.

"At least I'll last longer than you with your 5 shots nigga!" Ro said and we both laughed.

"You want a ride cuzz?" Asked Ro.

"Nigga you already know, I was finna say I'll smoke a blunt with you." I told him grabbing my bike.

"What, ya thought you was gonna ride for free? Let's roll." He said. I opened the back up and was careful to not lean my bike too much on the sub woofers Ro installed in his mom's ride. It may have been hers , but Ro really owned it.

I jumped in and Ro cranked the ride up and he had to turn the system down instantly.

"Where you get your bud at?" Asked Ro.

"Roc's. Why?" I asked pulling my dub sack out and started to break some down to roll up.

"Just asking. Did you pay cash or dick? Ha,Ha!" Ro said playing. Ro was the only person I ever told what happened between me and Peaches.

"Ha ha, naw, Roc was there and honestly I don't see that ever happening again. I got Reneé now." I told him.

"Go on with that lovey dovey shit nigga." Said Ro.

"Nigga ain't shit wrong with that. Not everybody can have 4 or 5 bitches like you Ro." I said.

"Whatever nigga, I learned from you. And now you a one-woman man, get the fuck on with that shit." Ro told me.

"Shut up nigga and spark that up." I said and passed the ball bat to Ro and he put his Bic lighter to it while I played DJ. I finally got to a track and me and Ro looked at each other and nodded our approval at the same time. Told you we was friends.

"Keep My Name Out Your Mouth"

By Big Pokey

Chapter 6

After a blunt and 15 minutes later we pull up to Reneé 's town house, she lived with her older sister and father. She must have heard the bass coming from Ro's Infinity cause I saw her pop her head through the curtain and pop back in.

"Aight Ro 'preciate it cuzzo. C safe bro, I'll holla atcha layta." I told Ro dabbing him up.

"Fasho. Get at me when you ready to bounce and I'll see if I can scoop you up." Ro told me.

"Bet. Love you man." I told Ro.

"Already my nigga, you already know." Ro told me.

I know what you may be thinking. These niggas on some gay shit. Nah man, it ain't nothing like that. When you got some people in your life you really cut for and are willing to give your own life up for that person, then they deserve the same three words you tell a bitch just cause she gave you a piece of pussy it applies to a friend too. In this game I've seen situations where people tell another person 'I love you,' but the other person can't respond 'cause they dead and can't talk back. By then its too late to really express your true feelings and to me its better to talk to somebody that talks back and not have a one-sided conversation. I got my bike out of Ro's ride and chunked the deuce and Ro was out of sight. I could still hear his system. I opened the gate in the back and rolled my bike into Reneé 's backyard porch. Reneé slid the glass door open and the curtain hung around her as I walked up. I could instantly smell her perfume or whatever she was wearing, all I know is that baby smelled good as hell! But what really got me is what she was wearing. O.M.G.! She was in a kimono and under it she had on a lace bra and panty set that made my jaw drop. She knew I approved 'cause she smiled. Reneé was fine as hell man, and I ain't just saying that 'cause she's my girl. She was 5'2" and thick. Legs and ass complimented each other perfect and she had a nice big rack , that was when you could tell she was Mexican. Hair dark brown, long and wavy and curled at the end that cuffed my finger tips. And as crazy as this may sound, what really turned me on the most was the color of what lil clothing she was wearing. Royal blue, my favorite color and she knew that too. It's the small things that really count so you got to pay attention. Life has taught me that.

"Hey mamacita. Damn girl you look good as hell baby" I told her and wrapped my arm around her waist and my other hand grabbed a big butt cheek. G-string not panties. Surprise, surprise. This just got better.

(Smooch, smooch)

"Hey papi, you like." Reneé asked in between kisses. I squeezed her in my arms tighter and caressed her even more.

"I'll take that as a yes?" She giggled. Muahz!

I never was into skinny girls, thick girls are where its at and baby was like a tea cup. Short and stout! I like meat in my soup and not bones, 'cause when I smack a girl's ass I don't want to worry about hitting bone, but all jelly. You dig?

I grab Reneé 's ass cheek and got her string on my thumb, I can't wait to use all I got on her tonight. We're both experienced and it's a good thing 'cause we ain't got to do any of that gentle shit. We finna make love porno style. And I'm going to pull all my tricks out and make it count, she'll never forget me.

My dick was hard and ready to pop out of my pants. Reneé didn't help when she reached and grabbed my shit. I felt her lips smile on mine. Approval.

I grab Reneé and toss her over my shoulder and she let out a yelp and small scream.

"Baby! You're going to drop me!" She said giggling.

"Never." I told her and carried her upstairs. We had the place all to ourselves. Her dad worked the night shift and her sister was somewhere probably doing the same shit.

Eventually I got to her room and gently tossed her on the bed and she bounced as well as her titties, one even popped and a nipple was showing. She was glistening from the lotion she had on and her legs showed the reflection of the lamp light and when her legs opened a lil I could see the fat of her pussy on the side. Bald. Just like I love it. I unbuckle my blue canvas belt and it clinks when it comes apart on my pants. Reneé 's eyes are glued to me and smiling and licking her lips and teeth. I only got my white beater and boxers on when I crawl on top of her and we began to lip fight. She bit me and I bit her, she sucked on me and I sucked on her. Damn, she had some lips.

I kiss her neck, licked on her ear and every time I did more her legs opened more for me. My dick was right on her pussy and I used my hips to move a lil bit side to side.

"Uh eshhh. Baby." She moaned.

"Mamacita." I whispered in her ear.

"Mmmm." She moaned

I kissed her neck and went down to her titties and kissed the both of them and then when I got her nipple in my mouth it drove her crazy.

"Ay papi. Eshhh! I love you Cris, mmmmm baby." She crooned. I felt my boxers getting me wet, Damn did she get wet. Or did I cum without knowing? Time to find out.

So, I slid my hand un between her thick legs and touched her pussy. Nope, I didn't cum, but baby was super fucking wet.

"Ah, ah baby." She moaned when I started playing with her clit.

"Uh, uh, uh. Shit papi. Mmm." She gasped.

I did that for a minute and got to my knees on the bed. Reneé 's eyes where damn near closed and glossy. I hooked my fingers to her G-string and peeled it off her and it felt cold from being wet and in a/c. I toss it and go down to her shaved pussy and take in the smell of her sex and loved the way she smelled. I put my hands on the back of her thighs and push them back towards her chest and her fat pussy is just there, wet and meaty. I start to devour her, taking her pussy in my mouth and my tongue went up and down going in and out in her pussy hole. She was

31

going crazy. Her hands were going everywhere and grabbing her pillows, grabbing her hair or touching her lips. She couldn't stay still, but it was a good thing. Guess I was doing something right.

"Uh, uh, uhm, ah! Baby! Baby, I'm coming. Uh." She cried out and I went harder and faster.

"I'm coming papi! Oh shit, eat your pussy! Eshh. Owww." She said in short breaths.

My face was all wet from her juices and she tasted like strawberry and a lil bit of honey.

I pulled back and grabbed her legs and turned her around with her fat ass in the air and her ass hole staring right at me

Smack

"Ah!" She screamed when I slapped her ass and ate her ass out. I smacked her one more time right before I entered her. My dick slid right in and she was super wet and very hot.

"Uh, uh, uh." She moaned with every pump I gave her. All you heard was me huffing and puffing, her moaning and our skins smacking all wet. About 5 minutes later I felt it coming.

"I'm coming baby," I panted.

"Cum for me daddy, cum in your pussy! Fuck this pussy!" She urged.

"Ahh, I'm coming baby."

"I'm coming too baby, keep going! Faster." She said and faster and harder I went.

"Uh, uh, ah, uh." We both said together.

"Ahh, shit!" I let it all out inside of her and gripped her ass and squeezed her cheeks so hard that when I let go my hand prints were still there. We lay there both panting and she lay on top of me and kissed my chest.

"I love you Cris." She told me.

I looked at her and grabbed her by the chin and kissed her.

"I love you too, Coconut." I told her and then I suddenly remembered about the box of condoms still in pants pocket.

Oh well, too late now.

"I Can Read Your Mind"

By Evant

Chapter 7

(Ring, ring, ring)

I woke up from my sleep in the dark. It was pitch black and I looked to my side and Reneé was still asleep. She was passed out. Especially after what we did for the past few hours. Shit, I was fucking tired.

(Ring, ring, ring) Oh yeah, that's why I woke up. I looked at her clock on the nightstand. 10:48pm.

"Who the fuck is calling?" I asked to no one in particular and then looked at Reneé . Still asleep.

(Ring, ring, ring)

Now she started to wake up. All of a sudden.

"Who's calling?" She asked me.

"I don't know, you tell me. The sancho?" I said sarcastically, but serious.

"Shut up babe, See who it is." And turned to get up and answer the phone.

"Hello" she said when she picked up the phone in mid ring.

"Yeah, he's right here, hold on. It's your mom." She said and passed me the phone.

"My mom? Hello." I said.

"Cris! Oh my God mijo." She said crying.

"Mom, calm down." I know Reneé heard her cause she got close to me and I can feel her and knew she was worried.

"Cris, they killed Lance! They killed him mijo." she said and continued to cry.

My mind went blank and only one thing came to mind. God giveth, God taketh.

Chapter 8

1993

    I was 6 years old and I was at my grandparents house on Eureka St. close to downtown. Both of my parents worked two jobs a piece so that they could support me and my sister that was almost a year old. We had everything we needed and then some, I guess spoiled is the right word. Plus our grandparents did the most as well, especially my grandpa. I was the oldest of his grandchildren so me and him were a lot closer. I had a cousin named Valencio, but I've been calling him Lance for as long as I can remember. He actually lived with our grandparents. My aunt Lilibeth couldn't get her shit fully together. She was the black sheep of the family, but she was really sweet with me.

    Me and Lance were super close, we were more like brothers than cousins. We was only two months apart and been sharing baby bottles and cribs since day one, inseparable. Until one day changed everything between us.

    We were running around our grandparents old house and my grandpa worked on big dumpster trucks for a living and had parts and tires everywhere. A semi junk yard to say the least. But for me and Lance it was the best playground in the world. Fuck monkey bars and slides!

"You can't catch me fat boy!" Screamed Lance ahead of me and I was huffing, trying to catch him. I knew I shouldn't have ate that extra bowl of Capt. Crunch.

"You're too slow!" Continued Lance and it was pissing me off, and then I see something and instantly come up with the greatest idea ever.

I jump on the tire that was laying on its side and I bounced on the bed of the truck and over the side of it and slam belly first on top of Lance. You should have seen his eyes bulge out of his head, poor kid didn't see it coming but it was too late. Gravity pulled me back to earth with a bang.

(Ka-Boom)!

I landed on Lance and we both went down.

"Oof! Ahhh. Get off me Cris! You fat meatball ! Get off !" he yelled. I was laughing really hard and he managed to push me off of him and I was on the dirt ground laughing still when he got up. He dusted himself off and scowled at me.

"You cheated!" He pointed at me and sneered.

"I ain't cheat!" I protested and got up.

"I got you fair and square. You're it!" I say and all of a sudden Lance pushes me. Now if I was skinny like him I might've fallen, but I barely moved back when he did push me.

"Cheater!" He yelled again.

"Take it back! I didn't cheat. Take it back!" I said to him not trying to fight, but what do you think a cat does when you corner it?

"You're fat, slow and stupid!" He throws insults my way. Now I'm starting to get upset.

"You better stop." I say warning him.

"Fat boy, fat boy, fat boy." He continues and I could only think of one thing to say that I have heard other kids say at school and it always got serious after that. Fuck it, I was upset by now.

"Yo momma!" I say to Lance and there went that look again and then rage.

Everybody knew aunt Lily had a sketchy past and Lance was aware of it all. He always had to listen to grandpa chastise his mom about always going out and meeting random guys. Lance never met his father and aunt Lily didn't really know who the boy's father was. Rage was in Lance's eyes and honestly it scared the shit out of me.

"Ahhh!" Screamed Lance and grabbed the first thing near him and tossed it at me. Ever see a chubby kid move fast? You should've seen me. Lance wasn't good at throwing a football, thank God. But when the soda glass bottle hit the rim right next to me, it shattered instantly.

(Crash)

I didn't feel it, the piece of glass sliced my cheek open so smooth and clean that if it wasn't for that face Lance made that I told you about with his eyes I wouldn't have known something was wrong. I looked around me first and then I felt coldness on my face and it started to sting a lil. I didn't think nothing at first, but when I touched my cheek and felt my fingers get wet and I looked at them all I saw was red. That's when I started whaling and hollering.

"Wah!" I yelled at the top of my lungs. I know that they heard me in heaven cause of how loud I screamed.

Seconds later my grandpa and grandma came around the corner, my grandma was still wiping her hands on her apron and then they went to her mouth.

"Ayi, Dios mio!" Said my grandma.

"What happened?" Demanded my grandpa and pulling a rag out his back pocket and coming to me. Everything happened so fast after that, I just remember everybody around me trying to stop the bleeding. and Lance just a stood there looking at me.

"Qué paso?" Asked my grandpa.

"It was an accident!" Said Lance.

"And ya had to cut him pendejo?" snarled my grandpa.

"Don't talk to him that way Jaimé!" Chastised my grandma.

"It was an accident he said". My grandma tried to defend Lance.

"Pinché guerco!" Cursed my grandpa.

"Hey! Don't talk to him that way dad. He's your grandchild too, remember? Or is Cris the only one?" Said Aunt Lily when she stepped out in her nightgown and hearing everything.

"Well if you wouldn't be out all night you would be able to pay attention to your son." Said my grandpa.

"I'm out all night working!" Said Aunt Lily in her defense.

"And laying on your back is what you call work?" Hollered grandpa.

"Jaimé!" Chastised grandma.

"You know what dad? I may not do things to your expectations but I am a good mother to Valencio and father!" She yelled.

"Ya! here Chenta hold this to his face while I go get the keys and take him to the hospital." said grandpa to grandma Vicenta.

"Quitate' pinche guerco bastardo!" Said grandpa shoving Lance to the side.

"Don't talk to him that way dad, and don't touch him!" Yelled Aunt Lily holding a teary eyed Lance.

We both looked at each other one last time for a long time while my grandma put me in the truck so I could get 6 stitches on my cheek.

"I ain't mad atcha"
By: 2-Pac

Chapter 9

Present

"Cristino!" My mom screamed my real name on the phone. That snapped me out of memory lane.

"Yeah mom, I'm here. Are you sure?" I asked my mom.

"Of course I'm sure! I've been here since Lily called me this morning. I am at the hospital. We had to identify his body. I'm on my way home now. I'll explain everything there. I love you mijo." She told me.

"I love you too mom." I said and hung up the phone.

"What happened babe? Everything o.k.?" Reneé asked and putting a hand on my back, kissing my shoulder. I finally turned the lamp light on and just sat there. It's like my body just had a mind of its own cause I got out of her bed and started getting dressed.

"Baby, where are you going?" She asked me sitting on her bed with her titties out. Damn, I hate that I had to go.

"Sorry baby, but I got to go" I told her still getting dressed.

"I can see that, but are you going to tell me why?" Asked Reneé . I cleared my throat before I answered.

"It's my cousin." I simply said.

"Your cousin? What cousin?" Asked Reneé confused.

"You never mentioned you had a cousin" She said.

41

"There's a lot you don't know about me." I told her.

"Obviously." She said upset.

"I'm sorry baby, I'll explain everything to you later, but right now I got to get home." I told her sitting on her bed to put my J's on.

"I understand papi." She tells me and grabs my face, turns it and kisses me so passionately. God how I wanted to get back in bed and ravish her again. It's like she read my mind and smiled, she even rubbed her thumb right over my scar. By now it was light and it healed great, no access meat.

"Rain check?" I asked after we kissed one more time.

"I'll be waiting to collect." She said and giggled.

"I love you Coconut." I told her.

"I love you too papi." And I left.

Chapter 10

All I thought about on my way home was how me and Lance became distant and how we didn't fuck with each other since our grandpa died. I had hate, regret and rage all going thru my mind and a couple of tears even came out of my eyes. I wish I could have been there for him I wish we was how when we was lil kids.

November 2000

Me and Lance was tighter than ever. We acted like nothing ever happened and we kept growing up together. We even made light of the situation and Lance gave me my first nick name. 'Scarface.' I was o.k. with it. We was thick as thieves, inseparable. Lance still stayed at our grandparents house, aunt Lily was still doing her. Not coming home for days at a time became normal eventually. When I would come around it would make Lance's situation worth baring. We had a blast together in the old neighborhood looking for anything to do, some good, most bad. By this time Lance really started to get involved with the street life which on the cool influenced me as well, and I was the oldest. Lance grew up faster than me, mom hardly there and no father. My parents were still together and both had a single job and we lived in the suburbs. But I felt things weren't always green.

Lance started to wear a bunch of blue and hung a blue bandana in his back pocket. I really didn't pay it no mind, until Lance told me his secret. He confessed to being a part of the gang 'Rollin Sixty Crips' and he was forealz about it.

My mom started to see the warning signs and didn't let me go around as much, but by that time a seed had been planted and it grew. Fast. One day Lance's life takes a worse turn, by this time we had stopped chillin for almost a year and it affected him.

One day Lance was on the metro on his way to his home boy's crib in the Heights, 20 minutes away. He was minding his own business when a group of kids in all red decided to fuck with Lance cause he was wearing too much blue for their taste. They were from Denver Harbor, another neighborhood close by that was infested with a gang called 'Lil Red. I'm sure you can guess what color they wore. I mean red everything, from the bandanas to the rosary's. Even the chicks with them were rockin the color.

One thing I forgot to mention about Lance was that my cousin gots a mean ass pull game. This fool had girls left and right, I mean why wouldn't he when his mom gave him the game on how to talk to hoes and what to say to get their attention. I ain't gonna, lie I watched him with a magnifying glass. Every time we would go to the mall he had a bitch by the hair while she had her mouth on his dick and didn't even know her name. True playa fareal! And the nigga was nothing but 13 fucking years old! All I had at the time was Manuela! Ain't that a bitch?!

Aimless Triggers—Jose C. Hernandez Jr.

Anyways, back to Lance and these clowns on the bus set trippin. In the group there was a chick who couldn't keep her eyes off of Lance, she even looked familiar to him, but he couldn't put his finger on it. Suddenly, she winks at him and Lance being Lance does the same thing back, but puts a smile with it.

Only it wasn't just the chick with eyes on Lance, one of the guys sees Lance wink and smile and didn't like it one bit. So he gets up and walks over to Lance. This kid was all skin and bones, maybe a buck soaking wet, but he swore to God he was a bad ass.

"Aye homes, you got a problem?" Asked Mr. Cholo.

"Say what foo?" Answers Lance back.

"I said" Started the kid, but Lance cut him off.

"I heard what you said playa. I meant it as rhetorical." Smart ass Lance said.

"And to answer your question. I was only admiring that pretty lil thang that keep staring my way." Lance gestured with his head and chin.

"Yo homes, that's my little sister and she ain't no lil thang." Said the kid with a sneer.

"I ain't mean no disrespect bro, chill out playa." Lance says putting his hands up with palms out cool as a fan. He moved a lil bit in his seat and felt the metal rub on the plastic seat.

"You better watch your back homie, you in the wrong side of town and got the wrong color showing." Threatened the kid.

"Ya got it bro, I ain't looking for trouble fam." "

45

" I ain't your fam homes." And then the kid walks back to his seat and wobbles from the bus moving.

Lance relaxes. It wouldn't have been his first time to bust his strap, but he wasn't trying to go that way. Not today. Not here.

The bus approaches a stop and the group of kids get up to get off, but ol' girl was the last one to get up and go. When she does Lance was watching her and she throws a piece of wadded paper at him and winks one more time and with her eyes basically tells Lance to pick it up. So he does.

On the paper it had the girls name (Josie) that included a phone number and (xoxoxo) Lance just smiles and put it in his pocket. A couple of days later Lance was going through his jeans looking for his zig zags and comes out with the piece of chewing gum paper Josie had put her info on.

"Oh shit" said Lance to nobody. He'd totally forgotten about it. Glad he found it tho.

He instantly got up and grabbed the house phone and dialed the number.

It rang twice.

"Hello?" said the girl. He liked her voice.

"What's good ma?" answered Lance.

"Who's dis?" asked Josie.

"Dang lil momma, how many other niggas did you give your number to on the bus?" asked Lance playing, but really hoping she didn't give him an answer he didn't like.

"He, he. Boy, stop. What took you so long to call? Scared of my brother?" she teased.

"Shit, you got me fucked up ma. My bad tho I got busy." He lied.

"Well I'm glad that you finally called, I thought I was never going to hear from you." She said that last part with a sad voice.

"Yeah my bad, but I wasn't too sure either, you feel me?" He said.

"Sorry about my brother, he's fucking stupid and overprotective." She told him.

"I understand ma, you're very pretty so I get it." said Lance smiling.

"My name's Lance by the way." He introduces himself.

"Is that short for something?" she asked.

"Valencio" he told her.

"Valencio?" she asked.

"Yeah." he felt a little embarrassed.

"I like it, it sounds better to me." She told him and giggled.

"I like the way you say it with the Spanish accent." He confessed, he was laughing nonstop for the rest of the phone call and it was on from there.

Three months later, Lance was chilling in the back of the house and hears a car pull up and stop fast on the gravel. He puts out his joint and goes to the front of the house and sees Josie get out of a car.

"Baby, who's car you in?" He asks Josie.

"Lance, papi we got to talk. It's important." She tells him.

"OK, but why didn't you just call?" He asks her.

"I had to see you face to face papi." She said and he saw fear in her eyes and was shaking.

"Yo mami, wassup? Tell me!" he tells her upset cause he don't like what's happening to his girl. To make matters worse, she starts crying.

"Come here baby." he pulls her in close and holds her tight.

"Now you're going to have to tell me what the fuck is going on girl cause you got me trippin'." He tells her and kisses her with both hands on her face.

"I'm pregnant." She finally tells him sniffling with tears in her eyes. Lance just looks deep into her eyes. He didn't want to believe it and his mind started to race. Even tho he had a bunch of hoes he always made sure to follow his momma's number one rule: Always use protection.

"It can't be baby, we always used a rubber, remember?" Lance said.

"Lance, remember that one time that the condom broke? Remember?" She said to him.

"Oh shit! you're right. But that was only one time." He said ignorantly.

"It only takes one time stupid!" Josie said and laughed.

"It's OK baby. I got you. I promise." He told her.

"I know. But I got to tell you something else babe." She said.

"What is it?" he asked.

"My brother knows. I told him when he found me throwing up and he took me to get a test from the store." She started crying again.

"He's on his way. I got here first cause I stole his car." She finished saying when a pickup truck pulled up and Josie's brother got out of the passenger side talking shit.

"Pinché maricon! You got my baby sister pregnant puto!" he yelled. *"I'm going to fucking kill you!"* he yelled some more.

"Pancho no!" Yelled Josie and ran to her brother to stop him, but he already had his gun out.

"Que esta pasando aqui?" Said grandpa Jaime coming out of the house. Before anybody could do anything a single shot was fired right before Josie was able to push her brother's hand to the side, but it was too late. Lance looked down at himself to see if he was shot and heard his grandma scream and Lance turned around quick.

He ran to his grandpa's side.

"Call 9-1-1 grandma! Go!" He yells at grandma Chenta.

"OK" she says.

"Grandpa?" Lance grabs his grandfather, he was wheezing.

"Lance." Said Jaime weakly.

"Don't talk Grandpa, save your strength. It's going to be OK." Lance told grandpa with a shaky voice.

"I need to tell you something." (Cough, cough.)

"It's OK Grandpa." said Lance.

"I'm sorry mijo. (cough) I'm sorry for everything." he wheezed more.

"I know grandpa, I know."   Said Lance with a tear falling down his cheek.

"I love you La." Was all Jaime said before dying.

The ambulance came and took grandpa away and the police took Pancho away. Me and my parents got there as fast as possible, but it was too late.

"Cris!" hollered Lance at me.

"What the fuck happened nigga?" I yelled at Lance. He broke down on what happened. I was full of rage and couldn't get my hands on the guy who was at fault. Instead I took my rage out on the one person I shouldn't have.

"I'm sorry Cris. I didn't mean for this to happen." Said Lance.

"Sorry? Sorry! you're always doing something to give the old man a hard time, but this time it got him killed." I say angry. I didn't give him a chance to say anything. "I hope you're happy. You never cared about him." I said.

"And he gave a fuck about me?" Lance finally said now angry as well.

"You know he did. That's the only reason he kept you and your mom around." I yelled really pissed off now.

"Well I guess he isn't the reason I stick around anymore, huh?' said Lance with hurt in his voice.

"I guess not nigga!" I spat back out.

"That's cool, you go your way and I'll go mine. Don't fuck with me ever again nigga." Lance said. Our feelings were getting the best of

us and we both said some shit we shouldn't have. But it was too late then and it's too late now."

"Pain"
By Z-Ro

Chapter 11

Present

Two Days Later (Friday)

Here I was, at the same funeral home we used for my grandpa two years ago, and now we're here with my cousin. This was actually the last place I laid eyes on Lance, throughout the whole memorial we stayed away from one another. You could feel the tension in the place, but out of respect for our grandfather, we kept the peace. Before it was our choice to part ways but this time God made the choice for us and if it wasn't too late before it's definitely too late now. I'm mad all over again, mad more at myself for rejecting Lances effort to reconnect with me. I'm a stubborn son of a bitch and now I'm here regretting so much. I feel like a hypocrite right now. When you see people crying at funerals it's not cause they're sad and genuinely going to miss the person that died, they're crying because of regret of some way or another. They regret that they won't be able to make peace with that loved one, regret is a motherfucker It's how I'm feeling about it right this moment. Death is something we cannot avoid, once God decides to pull your card and call you home you got no choice but to go. No "wait, let me say goodbye and I love you." Nah homie, it don't work like that. I sure as hell wish it did. Death just laughs at your sorrow with that rotten chipped grin on his face.

"Hey mijo." My mom snaps me out of my thoughts when she puts a gentle hand on my head.

I wipe the tears falling down my face.

"Hey mom." I look up at my mom. I could see she's been crying as well.

"How's aunt Lily? She OK?" I ask my mom.

"She's a mess." My mom says and blows air out of her mouth and sits next to me.

"What mother wouldn't be when she has to bury her child, it should be the other way around." She continued.

"I can only imagine if that was you mijo. First I lost my father, then my husband. I can't bare to lose you too." She said sniffling. Her hands were shaking and I hated seeing her this way. It brought questions to mind.

"Mom, God took grandpa and let dad leave us. You can't feel sorry for any of that. They teach us God is merciful, but how can that be with all that goes on here. I wonder if God is even real? Why does this God allow for all these bad things to happen?" I protested. My heart was in a dark place and somebody had to feel my pain. Anybody.

"God don't care about us. It's just a chess game between Him and the devil and guess who's winning?" I say with anger.

"Cris!" Don't say those things mijo. You know God loves you." My mom assures me.

"Well it's true mom, look at you crying and God is nowhere to wipe your tears away."

"He wasn't there when you cried in your room after grandpa died and when dad left." I throw in her face and continue.

"You begged and cried to Him to bring grandpa back, to bring dad back, but did God bring any of them back?!" I say loudly and angry.

(Smack!)

I didn't see it coming. This lady was fast.

"Don't you ever disrespect me again and don't use God's name in vain! Ever! You hear me pendejo? Never!" She yells at me and stands up.

"I am your mother and no son of mine will disobey God." Shit got real real quick.

"Why you slap me for mom? I'm the one that's been there for you by your side and never left. But you cry for those that have?"

(Smack) Again? Shit.

She trembled and shook.

"I guess I'll just do the same and leave. Maybe you can have a reason to cry for me as well." I say coldly and get up, I beat the concrete with my shoes. Hard.

"Cris! Wait! Where are you going? I'm sorry!" My mom was crying and screaming behind me, but I wasn't trying to hear shit. I had to go.

"As A Youngsta"
By: S.P.M

Chapter 12

A mile and a whole blunt later I was still upset. The blunt that I took to the dome didn't do a damn thing for me and I was out of cigars and down to my last few cigs. I stop at the nearest corner store. I don't recognize the area for shit, I've never been here in my life. My grandparents neighborhood and Alief was all I ever knew. In my angry trance I didn't pay attention to where I was going. Now I'm hot and sweaty, this humidity ain't helping. I'm in Northside somewhere on Antoine, that's all I knew. What I also knew was that I needed more cigars and an ice cold drink and fast.

I go inside the store and the blast of cold a/c is a relief to me and my legs felt cool. The starch in them made my legs hotter. I go straight to the soda fountain and grab the biggest cup and fill it to the top with ice and then some Mountain Dew. I grab a bag of Skittles (purple bag) and go back to the front. It wasn't an Arab like in my hood, this guy was Chinese and didn't smile for shit.

"Is that all?" Asked the chink. "

Can I get some cigarillos and a box of Marlborough mild?" I said with my best effort to sound grown and like I was old enough.

"ID?" he demanded. I acted like I was looking for it and patted myself down putting on my best effort to make it look good.

"Damn, I forgot it my man." I say and smile.

"No ID, no cigar." he says. "$1.65 for soda." he demands. Damn, no dice.

"Chill bro." I say patiently.

"I not yo bro!" He yells.

"Well give me a pack of zig zags then." I say to him.

"No ID, no tobacco." he continues.

"Man foo, ain't no tobacco in zig zags!" I protest."

"I no fool, you fool! I know why you want zig zag." He says. OK, you want to act like a hoe? Bet.

I shot out that door so fast that it caught that chino by surprise. I guess he's never seen a chubby kid like me move fast. In my hood you had to be or get stomped on.

"Hey You got to pay!" he yelled behind me, but I was gone! I could've paid for my shit, but fuck him. I ain't from around here and it was just a candy and soda. I ain't kill anybody.

I only run for a block and a half cause I got tired and slowed down. I looked back to see if anybody was chasing me. Clear. I see a pay phone and go to it and pop a quarter in. I ain't know where the fuck I was? All I know is that I had to move around fast!

I dial Reneé 's number first, just to check in. I kept cutting my eyes everywhere mostly cause I didn't know where I was, and because there was people going in and out of the shopping center.

Reneé picked up right at last ring.

"Hello," she sounded unsure of who was calling.

"Baby" I say happy to hear her voice.

"Cris! Baby where are you calling from?" she asked curious.

"On a pay phone somewhere in North Side. I don't know where I'm at? I'm close to the funeral home by Hempstead." I told her reading the closest street sign.

"Are you OK papi? Need me to come and get you?" She tells me worried. Baby was always ready to ride no matter what. Can't get them like that anymore.

"Yeah, I'ma call Ro, so just chill mami." I tell her.

I'ma go with him, let me 3-way him real quick." She said making her mind up. Can't argue with Reneé .

"Aight baby, but" I didn't finish saying what I was saying cause I was rudely interrupted.

"Say look out blood. What's up dawg?" said the voice and it gave me chills. Shit.

"Baby?" I heard Reneé calling me but I couldn't ignore the situation I just got put in and I had to face the voice talking to me. I couldn't pay attention to the phone cause I had a pressing matter at hand.

"Yo, what's poppin damu?" Said the black kid in all black with a hint of red here and there, a red bandana on his right wrist. I had a royal blue bandana in my back pocket and wore royal blue most of the time. I was part of (Insane Gangsta CRIP) and our colors were royal blue and yellow/gold. Bloods and Crips have been beefing forever.

"I said what's popping dawg, you know where you at blood?" he asks. I drop the phone receiver.

"I don't want any problems bro." I said, trying to plea bargain.

"You ain't from around here. I never seen an essay wearing so much flue before." he says being disrespectful.

"Naw, I'm just passing thru. I'm trying to get someone to come get me right now. I'll be out your way soon fam." I tell him. God please let me make it.

"Shit, you got yo rag hanging out like you want some trouble nigga. This blood territory dawg, and you got the wrong color showin'." He tells me and starts coming closer to me. I notice the chrome in his hand. Where did that come from?

Fuck.

"Yo man chill, I ain't trying to do all this." I plead. I'm fucked up that he got the drop on me. If I even try to reach for my gun I'll be dead before I even get a grip on it.

"Ain't no crab ass nigga gonna come to Acres Homes and get out alive dawg." he spat at the floor by me and stepping close.

What I did next I wouldn't recommend to anybody cause it won't always work. I just got lucky. I hit ol' boy with all I had and as fast as I could, he hit the brick wall behind him and his gun clattered to the floor. I hit him a gain and felt his face smash against my knuckles, his head bounced off the brick wall. The last punch was to his stomach, the three piece combo did what I needed it to do and he went down. I was never the type to kick a man while he was down. Like I said, I'ma give you action. In this case I should've gone to work on him. I tripped out. The guy's hand lands right on top of his pistol and I see that instantly. One word came to my mind. Run!

I took off so fast, but not fast enough. The sound of a gun going off was right behind me and it was loud. I cut around the corner of the building and just ran into some apartments all the while the guy's hand is roaring behind me. I saw the breaking of bricks right in front of me. He was blasting away and I was trying to avoid the bullets. He kept busting and busting. How many fucking bullets did he have?

I got to a porch gate and open it and stumble inside. I reach for my pistol and stay hiding. All the while the guy busted and then suddenly stops. It got super quiet and I stay still and wait. I heard a woman scream and continuous to scream. All of a sudden the door opens and a big lady comes out in her robe and sees me with a gun in my hand, screams and shuts the door back again. Smart lady.

I looked at my Fossil watch compliments of my dad. 1:45? Shit. It was still early and I was far away from home. I heard sirens and felt like that was my cue to move around.

Chapter 13

"Mmmm, damn girl. Suck that dick. Mmm". Moaned Ro as Cookie was giving him some fire ass dome.

Slurp gulp slurp slurp pop)

"You like this daddy? Said Cookie smacking Ros dick to her pink juicy lips (slurp, slurp)

"Hell yeah girl, Eshhh, ohhh yeah Ro said grabbing a hand full of Cookie's dirty blonde hair forced her down to go deeper inside her mouth.

(gag, cough, spit)

"Ah!" Yelped Cookie when Ro's dick came out of her mouth full of saliva.

"Fuck me daddy". Crooned Cookie and stood up and dropped her thong. Turned around and sat on top of Ro's dick and slid down in one motion.

"Shit, mmm. Fuck girl. Ride that dick baby, yeah just like that. All you could hear was Cookies ass :smacking on top of Ros body.

"Uh, uh, uh. Shit baby. She screamed in pleasure. Her double DD titties. just bounced up and down with every stroke Ro gave from under her.

(Ring Ring) (Ring, Ring)

Ro heard his cell Ringing even tho the music was on + Cookie making all that Noise from the pleasure she was receiving.

Fuck that phone, he thought to himself. His priority was busting a Nut in Cookies tight, wet pussy. Even after all these years her pussy was as tight as when he first popped her cherry when they was 12. Cookie's Real name was Lizzy, she was thick in a skinny white girl way. Usually you didn't see too many white girls with thighs and ass. Cookie was raised around Mexican's So I guess you can say them tacos did her right, not your average bimbo.

She had Mexican in her some how. Literally speaking at this very moment.

"I'm coming! Fuck - this pussy daddy! Oh fuck I'm coming! She yelled and that. did it for Ro

"I'm coming baby. Ah shit! Ahhh! Screamed Ro-loading himself inside. of Cookie Cookie gets off Ro's dick, stands up and faces her man and her big titties just swivel. Ro couldn't help but grab her and pull her towards him and pops one of her big pink nipples right into his mouth and begins to suck.

"Mmm" Moans Cookie.

(Ring ring) (ring ring)

His phone begins to go off again.

"Your phone's ringing babe." He loved Cookie. She didn't ask any questions that other bitches would usually ask. She knew she was his and only his and that was good enough for her even if he did have other bitches. None of them could knock them off of her throne next to Ro.

"Fuck that phone, I'm busy." he says and plays with Cookie's cookie. (ring ring) (ring ring) OK now the phone got his attention. He stops fondling Cookie enough to get up and go get his phone. She lays on the bed and Ro comes back and lays next to her and proceeds to rub her coochie and answer the phone at the same time.

"What?" he answers irritated.

"Henry!" said Reneé calling Ro by his birth name.

"Reneé , sup?" Now he stopped finger fucking Cookie all together.

"Wait, slow down, what happened?" Asked Ro and got up to start getting dressed. Cookie got up on her elbow and continued Ro's job by herself.

"You sure? OK I'm on my way. Bye." Ro said hanging up and then he turned to explain to Cookie that he had to go, but her eyes were closed and legs wide open while she played with her pussy. Ro hated that he had to leave Cookie like this, but she had things under control so he didn't feel so bad. She'll be alright, but his homie needed him. Pussy came and went. Cookie knew Ro's lifestyle and respected whatever he did. She knew a lot about Ro's business cause Ro pillow talked with her too damn much Cookie knew too much if you asked me and I told Ro to be careful what he told her, but he said he trusted her. But I didn't. There was something sneaky about the bitch. Especially when I would catch her looking at me a certain kind of way sometimes. Bitches only knew what they knew cause a nigga would spill more than just a nut on her and to me that was a no-no. That's why so many good niggas got took down in my hood cause he couldn't keep his mouth closed to an open pair of legs. Real talk.   "Regulators" By: Warren G. fl. note Dagg

62

Chapter 14

"Whatcha got Det. Riviera?" asked senior detective Jeff Goodman stepping out of his unmarked Crown Victoria Interceptor.

Det. Lorenzo Riviera, his partner of 8 months had just finished interviewing witnesses. Goodman had 25 years with HPD/Homicide division and was ready to finally retire in 4 months. He was training young Det. Riviera to take his place. Goodman was 45 years old and tired of all that shit going on in the streets of Houston. And it was only getting worse by the day. Riviera was young, fresh, and determined. With a lot of potential of becoming a great detective. Goodman just hoped the kid had the stomach for it, it wasn't easy work after all. Goodman lost a lot of sleep because of the images burned to his mind and he could never find a way to get rid of them no matter the name that was on the bottle he drank from. After 2 ex wives and a kid Goodman had started to give up hope. With alimony, child support and bills piling on top of one another, the pressure was only getting worse. He put 25 years into the streets of Houston in trying to clean them up and what did he get in return? A slap in the face, that's what. It was time to let some other schmuck do it, he was done. He did his best and put as many gang bangers, murderers, rapists behind bars and was sincerely proud of it. But it was getting old and he was getting old. He was tired.

"Regina Morris black female 8 years old. Lived with a single mother and had an older brother. Mother's name is Shaniss Morris and her brother's name is Brandon Morris. The father is serving a life sentence for an armed robbery that turned into a homicide. Mrs. Morris was pregnant with Regina at the time the bank was being robbed and things went sour fast." Finished Riviera reading from his notes.

"I remember that case, winter of '91 correct?" Stated Goodman.

"Correct sir. You were involved?" Asked Riviera.

"No I wasn't. I just know the facts. The father got life for not cooperating against his codefendant who was the one who actually killed the woman teller. She was the same one who pushed the panic button." Finished Goodman.

"Correct again, sir." Said Riviera.

"What else?" asked Goodman heading to the actual crime scene and going into an apartment on the side of the building. There was a lot of people out.

"I was able to find out that her brother is part of a gang. The 59 Piru gang. A branch of the Bloods. He's 18 years old and goes by the name…"

"B-Mo." Goodman finished for Riviera.

"Correct Sir, but how do you know that?" Asked Riviera curious as they went under the yellow "Caution" tape.

"He and his gang are suspect in a number of homicides and robberies around the area. This is their territory from I-10 all the way to 290 up and down Antoine." Said Goodman, looking around the room and saw the lifeless body under a white sheet on the floor. Toys were still in the same position they were left in, where little Regina, played with them.

"Have you spoke to the mother?" Asked Goodman

"Yessir. I saw the older son leave with a group of guys, he was gone before I could stop him. I got a feeling this isn't over, not yet anyways." Said Riviera, he had a daughter as well. Same age as a matter of fact, he couldn't imagine what he would do if something like this happened to his baby.

"It usually doesn't with drive by's" Said Goodman.

"That's the thing Sir, it wasn't a drive by. A lady reported to seeing a boy on the patio hiding and holding a gun. She heard the shots and came out to see what the fuss was about and saw the boy" Stated Riviera.

"Did she give a description?" Asked Goodman, now focusing on his partner.

"Yessir! Hispanic male, mid-teens, wearing alot of blue, but nicely dressed. Her words. Clothes look expensive she said, and he was wearing "robot pants". Riviera finished quoting.

"Robot pants?" Asked Goodman now confused.

"Starch. His pants had heavy starch. Sir." Said Riviera.

"Go on." Said Goodman.

"Uhm. About 5'10", a little on the heavy side and really handsome. Again, her words." Finished Riviera.

"You said he had a gun right. It's what the witness said. Correct?"

"Yes. She described it as 'a cop gun. The old one's that spin'." Said

Riviera.

"A revolver I assume she meant?" Asked Goodman

"Correct. I verified by showing her my pistol I got on my ankle strap." Stated Riviera.

"But I saw the marker's for bullet casings on the street. Ten of them if I counted correctly." Said Goodman

"I noticed that as well." Said Riviera.

"So we may have two suspects." Goodman spoke.

"It seems as so Sir." Agreed Riviera.

"Two possible shooters. The autopsy will confirm what caliber ended the child's life." Said Goodman.

"As a matter of fact, yessir." Said Riviera

"Ok, call me as soon as you know for certain. I got a funny feeling about all of this and it doesn't make sense." Said Goodman walking back to his car.

"They never do sir." Said Riviera on his partner's heels.

Goodman opened the car door and got in, but before shutting the door he spoke to Riviera.

"Good job Detective, keep up the good work! And shut the door, crank the car on and peeled off.

"Thank you Sir." Said Riviera to no in particular.

Chapter 15

"Welcome to McDonald's, how may I take your order, young man?" Said the over-weight black lady behind the counter.

"Yeah, can I get a McGang-Bang please and large fries and drink?" I ordered

"A McGang-Bang? I've never heard of such thing." Said the lady, puzzled.

"What? Forrealz?" I asked sarcastically. She gave me that "Do I look like I'm playin" look.

"It's a Hot-N-Spicey and Double McCheese burger put together in one." I tried explaining to the lady that I was surprised never heard of such a great combination.

"You do know that's two different burgers and I'm going have to charge you for them both right?" She told me.

"That's cool, thanks." I told her. I was fucking starving.

"That will be 4.28" She told me.

"I can't believe you've never tried it before." I tell her trying to make light of the conversation.

"No I haven't. I can tell you've been eating them for a while now." She clowns on me and looks me up and down.

"Bitch!"

I snatch my change, grab my cup and head straight to the fountain. I could hear big momma explaining to her co-worker my order.

"Oh yeah, girl that's really good!" I could see the lady look at me with a stupid look on her face and just smile. "Yeah bitch."

I go sit down and wait on my order, but didn't wait long.

"Order #78." Yelled the lady.

"Oh that's me. Yessir!

I got my order, sit at the front by the counter and t.v. and began to mow my fries down first. I was super hungry. I was just about to take a big bite of my burger – when the news on the t.v. got my attention.

Breaking News!

The volume wasn't high, but clear enough. A reporter pops up on the screen.

"Yes Eric, neighbors say that the shooting happened right behind me across the street from this little strip of a shopping center at those apartments." The lady was saying. I recognized them apartments instantly. Shit, the same spot I was hiding at was right there on t.v. I stopped eating and listened.

"According to the witnesses, one of the alleged gun men was hiding inside one of the apartment's gated porch. The suspect that was hiding was seen with a gun in his hand. It is not clear whether or not he is actually responsible for the death of 8 yr. old Regina Morris." They showed a picture. I see all smiles.

"Shit!"

"Family and friends are mourning... This young innocent girls life that ended violently by the hands of two reckless individuals gunning it out in the..."

"Two reckless individuals?"

"One suspect is described to be about 5'10", mid teens. About 200 lbs, Hispanic with very close cropped haircut. He was last seen in a blue patterned dress shirt and dark blue jeans." She described me.

This individual is wanted for questioning by the authorities. He is presumed dangerous, so don't approach the suspect. Call the local authorities or TIPS hot line." She was saying.

I was in shock. Did they think I killed that lil' girl? I didn't even bust my gun. What the fuck? I couldn't believe this!

"Hey, you him aren't you." Somebody behind me said and I turned in my seat. Saw that it was the old lady at the counter.

"I didn't kill her." I said more to myself than to her.

Her eyes went wide.

"It is you." She says and runs to the back.

"Somebody call 9-1-1. The shooter is right here. Call 9-1-1!" She screamed.

"I didn't do anything." I say getting up off my chair.

"Help! Somebody help!" She kept screaming.

I got up out of there quick. Damn man, it's like I've been on the run a lot lately. God damn!

(Ring)

"Goodman". Answers the detective.

"Where?" He exclaims.

"On my way." He says and punches the gas and turns his siren on.
About ten minutes later he pulls up to the McDonald's. Gets out of the
car and walks in. Sees his partner in the back and goes to him.

"Tell me you got something?" He told his partner

"We got footage of him at the counter, a clear view of his face." Said
Riviera

"Show me." Said Goodman.

Riviera pushes play and the video runs. They both watch the whole thing
carefully and when it stops Goodman addresses his partner.

"Could be him. I want you to show this to Mrs. Dukes at the apartment
and see if you can verify it's him. Contact me as soon as you get a
positive I.D. If it's him we'll then run his face on the 9 o'clock news
tonight." Ordered Goodman.

"Yessir." Riviera said, getting up and Goodman just stared at the frozen
image on the screen.

"I'ma get you." He said to himself.

Chapter 16

"We gotta get that crab mother fucker!" Said B-Mo to his homeboys that
surrounded him at his trap house he had.

"Fa'sho." One guy said.

"I'ma rip that flue rag out his pocket and choke him with it!" Said
another.

"Yo homie. I'm sorry, Damu." Said Damion.

Nobody knew it was him that was there shooting.

"He should be dead right now and not my sister." Snarled B-Mo when he
addressed Damion.

B-Mo and Damion been homies a long time. Both of their fathers were
O.G. Bloods from back in the day. Damion's father was with B-Mo's
father when they robbed the bank 9 years ago. There were rumors that
Damion's father didn't want to take responsibility for killing that white
lady and B-Mo's father didn't turn state snitch on Damion's father. He
believed that the G code to the fullest. After their father's arrest B-Mo
and Damion stuck together, but truth be told B-Mo started to notice a
change in Damion – wasn't sure if he could trust his home boys fully
anymore. Only Damion and the fool he busted at really knew what
happened earlier.

Damion was determined to find that Mexican and kill him before it all
came to light. Damion couldn't have that.

"I'm sorry fam. On Piru, I'ma be the first to kill that crab mother fucker."

Damion voiced.

"No. I want him alive! I want the pleasure in killing him slowly and painfully." He says this to the whole crowd.

Damion had other plans.

Chapter 17

Around 10 o'clock later that day

"Damn my nigga". I said opening the door to my ride that just barely picked me up.

"I thought I'd never be saved bro!" I continue to tell Ro.

"Bro, you took forever to call back and yo dumb ass don't know how to give good directions!" Ro shot back at me irritated.

"Man foo' I've had a crazy ass fucking day and it was one thing right after another, back to back." I was saying talking fast as Ro took off.

"I couldn't catch a fucking break cuzz!" I'm finally safe and fall back into the leather seat of the luxury truck.

"Here, I know you need this." Ro says and passes me a fat ass blunt the size of a real cigar. Did he just empty it and stuff it without cutting the motherfucker?

I grab it, spark it and take a long ass pull without hesitation. I take a couple of long pulls before I try passing it back to Ro.

"Nah bro. That's all you. Take it to the head, I'm straight right now." He tells me and tries to navigate out of this hell hole.

(Inhale, exhale) Repeat. Once Ro figured out which way we had to go and get to I-10 heading south, he relaxed.

"So what happened bro. Run it down." Ro said getting on the ramp and punching the gas.

"Cuzz". I was already high as a plane by now. I started unloading my day off on Ro. All he did was drive, trying to concentrate on the road. Swanging and swerving lane to lane, smashing on the gas.

I told him everything that happened from the beginning. From me and my mom getting into it, to me hiding in the abandoned car wash waiting for the sun to go down.

"Why ain't you bust slob ass nigga cuzz?!" Ro says mad at me.

"My nigga! Didn't you hear anything I said? That nigga had the drop on me! I couldn't do nothing other than what I did do and it worked, or else I wouldn't be here telling you my story, right?" I protested.
"Aight, aight. Chill. Don't hit me too bro." Ro says fucking with me.

"Ha ha!" I laughed.

"I'm glad you OK tho fam, you good now. Well let me rephrase that, you good for right now. Reneé has been worried about you and been blowing my cell up non stop." Just as Ro said that his cell rung.

"Speaking of the devil." He says, looks at the caller ID and tries passing me the phone.

"I don't want to talk to her right now. She's gonna be cussing me out and shit. I'll just text her." I say and grab the phone.

(On the way back, driving) Send.

"So, they got Valencio? Reneé told me." Ro finally asked.

I ain't spoke to Ro since the day he dropped me off at Reneé 's house.

"Yeah man." I say and look out the window. It was dark so I really wasn't looking at shit, just looking and thinking.

"Fuck cuzz, sorry to hear about that. I never met 'ol boy, and you hardly talked about him and I know what I know about him when you bring him up from time to time." Ro said, reminding me.

"Yeah well, he's gone now. I don't know what to really feel? A part of me wants to cry, but the other part of me don't let me." I say sincerely.

"So what are you going to do cuzz?" Asks Ro.

"About what?" I ask.

"Locs, a little girl is dead and you're wanted for questioning. The news basically said it was your fault the lil girl is dead cuzz." Ro tells me.

"Fuck man." I say leaning and putting my face in both my hands and rubbing my face with frustration.

"I don't know bro?" I say behind my hands.

"Where's your gun?" Asked Ro.

"Get rid of it." Ro said.

"Get rid of it? You crazy nigga?" I say with attitude.

"You say you didn't pop off a round, but if they catch you with a gun they'll put more charges on you bro." Ro says.

He's been to juvie before so he knows more about the system than I do.

"Ro, I didn't shoot and regardless with or without a gun they still gonna try to hang me. I'd rather go with my feet on the ground than on my knees!" I say.

"Alright,, you know what you're doing cuzz. I got your back, remember that." Ro says.

"I already know." I tell him.

"So where to?" Asks Ro.

"I'ma need some money and fast 'cause lawyers are expensive " I tell him.

I had a few grand stashed, but a few grand wasn't going to pay for a good attorney an ain't shit was happening 'till I get a really good lawyer. Fuck court appointed lawyers! There went my slab I was saving up for, no 84 spokes or candy paint. No nothing! Thank you, snoop ass nigga.

"So do I make the call or what?" asks Ro, breaking me out of my thoughts.

"Yeah, call him." I say and pass Ro his phone.

He scrolls thru his contacts and presses call and waits a few seconds.

"Yo Rico! What's up fam?" Ro says into the phone.

"Yeah, yeah. Good my nigga. Say, me and Locs need to pull up on you. You free?" Ro asks and listens.

"Alright bet. See you tomorrow morning then. Deuce." And Ro hangs up.

"Alright we on for tomorrow." He tells me and puts his cell down.

"To Reneé 's?" Asks Ro this time.

"Naw, yo crib. I need a shower and a change of clothes. I'll call her." I say.

"Your funeral homie." He says and turns up the stereo.

"Rollin' On Swangaz"

By Z-Ro ft. Chris Ward and lil Keke.

Chapter 18

The Next Day - 7:15am (Saturday)

Det. Goodman came and sat with his cup of black coffee, still hung over.

"So what do we know partner?" Goodman says taking a sip of coffee. He still had his aviator shades on. Riviera noticed and just sighed.

"Well, we know she was as healthy as any normal 8 year old would be, so her death was not caused by natural causes." Said Riviera and looked at Goodman.

"Oh, we got a smart ass today huh?" Goodman said and finally took his shades off.

"It's too early for all this. Can you give me a break and facts, please? Thanks." Said Goodman tossing his shades on his desk and went back to his coffee.

Riviera sighed again and continued a little irritated.

"Regina was shot and killed by a ,357 caliber bullet. The casings found at the scene were a positive match. The casings were ejected out of a .357 glock SIG suer, not a revolver. So that tells me that the kid that the neighbor saw didn't cause for little Regina's death per se', but he was still involved." Stated Riviera matter of factly.

"We still need to find him, he's the only one we got a description of and maybe if we squeeze hard enough we can get him to co operate with us and tell us who was the other asshole who wanted to have a shoot out in the middle of the street." Said Goodman.

"I couldn't agree any better partner." said Riviera.

"Have we got a clue as in who this kid is yet?" Goodman was the senior detective but technically this was Riviera's case. Goodman was just basically over seeing the case by monitoring Riviera and making sure his protege did everything by the book. So far so good.

"Well I was going to that next. Mrs. Burke's identification of the suspect puts us at an advantage. She was able to confirm that the photo I showed her was indeed the same kid that was at McDonald's, we can run his face thru the data system. But being that he's a juvenile he might not even have a record or committed a crime that's gotten him fingerprinted and took a photo on.." Said Riviera.

"Uh-huh." Goodman said waiting to see where his partner was going with this.

"Another option we have is scanning the photo we do have of him and e-mail it to every school in the district and hope to get a hit. He had to go to school around here. The lady at the register said that when he left he left on foot. So he has to be from around the area." Finished saying Riviera.

"That's not a bad idea partner. It just may work. I say we do that and hope for the best and if we have to widen the areas of districts then we will." Says Goodman getting up off his chair and stands to leave.

"Where you going?" Asks Riviera. "To get more coffee. It seems we got a long day ahead of us buddy and I need a bigger boost of energy." Said Goodman.

"Yeah, I bet." scoffed Riviera.

"Nobody likes a wise guy" Shot back Goodman and he left for the break room.

"Did you give your connection at the news station the picture last night?" asked Goodman just remembering.

"Yeah I did but by the time I got to Mrs. Burks and to the news station it was too late. It'll be on this afternoon for 12 o'clock." says Riviera. "

OK good. Good job partner." Said Goodman and left.

Chapter 19

8:20am.

I woke up the next morning on Ro's couch and Cookie was in the kitchen cooking breakfast. Hoes can be housewives, I guess. It did smell good and I'm a sucker for breakfast so I gots to get some grub.

"Morning" I say to Cookie passing her by. She only had two pieces of clothing on and it didn't cover much of the top or bottom.

"Hey" She said and looked at me. Let me be clear, me and Cookie would have been fucking a long time ago. The only reason Ro ended up having her was 'cause I didn't choose her. I mean she was fine. But I just didn't want to fuck with her I had a feeling about the bitch and I usually follow my gut. I ain't chubby for no reason. There have been instances where we would be partying and if Ro was not paying attention she would shimmy her way towards me and make a move on me. She even grabbed my dick one time and confessed to me that she wished me and her had hooked up instead of her and Ro. Ro's my best friend and I couldn't disrespect my boy like that. I always put a stop to her flirtatious comments and gesturing and never told Ro anything 'cause I know more than likely he'd kill the bitch. I just didn't feel like being in the middle of that shit, but Ro knew I wouldn't cross the line, it is what it is.

"Where's Ro?" I asked.

"Showering, He said ya'll was going to see Rico." She said stirring eggs.

See what I mean? Why do niggas got to tell their bitch everything?!

"Hmm" I just say and leave it at that. I definitely ain't fucking the bitch so why do I got to tell her what I got going on?

"Wussup Locs" Ro says coming into the kitchen showered.

"What's good?" I say and dap my homeboy up.

Cookie drops two plates on the table and me and Ro get to work.

"Yo Ro, I need to borrow some gear cuzzo." I tell Ro in between bites.

"You already know wussup nigga. Get what you need." He says with a mouthful.

"What's the plan?" He asks.

"Same as last night." I say and leave it at that and continue to grub.

I finish my plate and go shower. I pick out my choice of clothes and get dressed. It's a good thing me and this nigga both got the same taste. Only piece of clothing item I still wore that were mine were my all black mid top Polo boots.

<u>An Hour Later</u>

We get to Rico's crib and could hear the bass from the reggaeton music playing on the house stereo system. We knocked and knocked, but no answer.

"Man text this nigga and tell him we at the door! It's too hot for this waiting outside bullshit." I tell Ro aggravated.

Ro texted Rico's number and a minute later a fine thick black girl answers the door. Puerto Rican honey's are fucking fine in every color.

"Pasale' ." She says and steps to the side and smiles.

Rico had a gang of stripper hoes that he used to break niggas off. You had the dope and money best believe Rico was going to send one of his bitches after you and get you for everything he could get you for. I know 'cause I've gone with him a few times before. Same reason we're here now.

"Oye' que lo que aye'?" Said Rico greeting us in his Puerto Rican accent from the sofa he was sitting on with two more fine hoes damn near butt naked next to him smoking a blunt. Nigga had gold all over him.

"Yo Rico, what's crackin' cuzz?" I say fucking with my boy.

Rico was a Latin King and was a shot caller in his circle. After popping a dude in New York he left and came down to Texas and has been terrorizing the strip clubs ever since. Being a bouncer is what got him to where he's at today.

"Oye', pero que lo qué tu dices carajo?" He tells me in Spanish and we shake hands and Ro does the same.

"Rico, you gonna let me sit by myself or what bro?" Ro tells Rico.

"Aye mami, dale' atencion ah ese cubron." He orders one of the chicks to go sit with Ro.

"Estas bien?" Rico asks me.

"I'm good bro." I tell him.

"You in love carajo?!" Rico makes fun of me.

"No disrespect Rico, but as fine as these ladies are, they ain't fucking with my Coconut." I say in defense.

"Ora, ora. I don't mean no disrespect Locs." He says laughing and raising both of his hands. We both start laughing.

"So what can I do for ya'll?" He asks us.

"Well actually, it's just for me." I tell Rico and he focuses on me.

Ro's chopping it up with 'ol girl on his lap and she's giggling her ass off.

"Yo Ro, you wanna take Luna to the other room so me and Locs can talk?" Rico says to Ro.

Ro already knows that he ain't going to miss out on what we are going to talk about 'cause he knows I'll lace him up later. I love my bro but I don't need him hearing everything so he could go back and tell Cookie. Me and Rico have spoken about keeping what we talk about between us only when it's about me. He understood.

After Ro and Luna left we continued.

"Dimelo. How can I help my Locs?" he says sparking a blunt.

I run down what happened yesterday bit by bit. I ain't had shit to hide and trusted Rico to the fullest. So I layed it all down and explained how I was going to need some serious cash and fast. He just nodded his head, listened and smoked away. After I was finished breaking it all down to him and stopped talking is when he finally let me hit the blunt. I puff on the blunt while Rico takes in all I just told him and thinks.

"O.K., so." He finally says.

"This means that the laws are after you. I saw on the news yesterday when they brought it up, but didn't think nothing of it.

"Estas jodido cabron." Rico says.

I know bro, that's why I came to see you. I need to make some bread and fast." I tell him.

"I really ain't got shit like that right now bro, but I still can help you make some easy money. It's a lot more riskier, but the pay is good." He tells me.

"What is it?" I ask curious.

"I got a shipment of coca coming in from Peru through Mexico. I need that shipment to get to my primo in Nueva York. I'll pay you ten g's to drop it off." He tells me.

"Damn bro." I say rubbing my chin.

"Look Rico. You know I respect you bro, I really do. But I ain't no mule homie and I appreciate it fam. I really do." I tell Rico.

"No, está bien. Yo entiendo. That's just what I got right now bro." He says to me sincerely.

Rico got a sad look on his face 'cause he wants to help.

"Check it yo. On the cool they don't got your name or nothing, so you're really good right now." He says and gets up and goes to a safe behind a picture frame.

"Here" he hands me a bag with coke in it.

"Take that. Sell it and get some change. If you decide to make that trip for me get back at me." Rico tells me.

"Preciate it bro, I'll pay you back as soon as I sell it." I tell him.

"Get on your feet bro. It's all good. Holla at me when you decide You're ready." Rico told me.

"Alright bro." I say and we slap hands.

"Stay On Your Grind" By: S.P.M.

Chapter 20

Me and Rico chopped it up for a few minutes more while Ro took care of his business with 'ol girl. My nigga was a big trick and didn't mind supporting a woman's hustle, especially when they was fine and exotic.

"Have you even called her?" asked Ro once we were back in his truck.

"Yeah at your crib last night." I told him referring to Reneé .

"So wassup?" He asks me, referring to my talk with Rico.

"Shit, he got some shit lined up cuzz, but I really ain't feeling it." I told Ro most of what we talked about and he knew why I didn't jump to it.

"Yeah man, just chill. Something will pop up eventually." He told me.

"I already know." I said and we drove with the music bumping and didn't say much else.

"Ambitions of A Rider"

By:2-pac

I get dropped off at Reneé 's and she's at the door by the time I get there. I go in for a kiss, but get something else instead.

(Slap)

"Damn babe, what was that for?" She ain't slap me that hard so I didn't really trip.

"Why didn't you come straight here last night Cris? You had me fucking worried." She tells me and I grab her. This time I got a kiss.

"Baby, I'm here now I can leave if you want." I say pulling away. She pulled me back and kissed me. Hard. I picked her up from her ass and carried her to her room.

"Where's your dad?" I asked kissing her.

"At his girlfriends." She said and we kissed more. We get to her room and it smells of candles and her perfume. I close her door with my foot behind me and drop her on her bed. I wasted no time and got up out of my clothes. She did the exact same thing. I crawled on top of her and go straight for her tittie, the one with the piercing I dared her to get. And she did it for me.

"Ahh baby." I heard her whisper.

I played with her titties back and forth, putting her nipples in my mouth one at a time and flicking each other while my hands kept rubbing her pierced nipple. It was driving her crazy.

"Ahh, eshhh." She exclaimed.

I then get on my knees and then lay down on my back.

"Put that pussy on my face baby." I tell her and she sits on my face sixty-nine style. I start licking her clit while she sucks my dick.

"Mmmm," I groaned in my throat when she wraps her hot mouth around my dick. She moans as I put my big mouth on her pussy.

"Hm, hm, hm." I suck on her clit and flick it with my tongue and she moans softly.

(Smack)

I slap her on that big juicy ass.

"Mmhmm." She yelps.

I reach around her booty and start finger fucking her wet coochie.

"Oh shit baby." She moaned when my finger went in.

I licked and finger fucked her at the same time while she slurped and gagged on my dick.

(Smack)

I loved smacking her on the ass, she had a lot of it. We sucked and licked nonstop. I let her make the next move. She got off my face and laid on her back, she played with her pussy as I got to my knees and crawled in between her legs.

"Fuck me papi." She cooed to me.

"I'm gonna fuck the shit out of you mamacita." I tell her.

I grab the back of her legs behind her thighs and push them all the way to her chest. Pussy all out for me, hairless and super wet. I enter her in one motion, fuck going in slow.

"Ahh!" She yelps and put's her palms on my chest, but doesn't stop me. I continue to go all the way in and let my dick lay inside of her.

"I love you chiquita hermosa." I tell her and kiss her.

"Te' amo papi." She moans.

I start pumping slowly and she moans with pleasure with every pump I give her. I cradle her and get even closer to her and get ready to start pounding. Once I was sure she wasn't going to move anywhere I got to putting work in. I pounded away so hard inside her pussy that she was screaming like I was killing her.

"Ah, ah, ah,ah! Fuck me!! Fuck me!! Uh, uh, uh!"

She was getting it and she loved it. I felt my dick and balls getting wetter and wetter. My balls were smacking her ass asshole with every stroke.

"I'm coming papi. I'm coming." She screamed.

"Cum for me. Cum on this dick girl!" I tell her and pounded even harder. Her whole bed shook and the headboard banged like thunder.

"Uhhh" She said with pleasure. Her leg started twitching and she was making noises in her throat that I didn't think she could make.

"Hmmm!" I huffed as I got ready to bust.

"Ah, shit baby! I'm finna nut! I'm coming! Ahhh. I let it all go in her.

I pull my dick out spank her pussy with it.

(Smack, smack, smack, smack, smack.)

"Mmm. That was great papi." She tells me heaving and we kissed. That was just round one.

"Sweating"

By Twista

Chapter 21

12 o'clock.

'Breaking News'

"Authorities have finally been able to obtain a photo from a video recording that was filmed at a McDonald's establishment close to where the gruesome murder of 8 year old Regina Morris took place two days ago." Said the anchor woman on screen of the camera.

"That's correct Cindy, HPD has reason to believe that this is a person of interest and is wanted by police for questioning in relation to the shooting." said the anchor man.

The camera cut back to the woman.

"Police have yet been able to put a name with the photo that we have been provided with. We are counting on the good people of Houston to help us identity this suspect and bring him to justice and hopefully get some answers and closure for little 8 year old Regina Morris." the anchorwoman said.

"I sure hope so Cindy. So if anyone has any questions please contact your local authorities or Hot TIPS line with the number provided." he said. They broadcasted the picture with the 'wanted' word over it and a number to call.

"I sure hope that worked." said Det. Goodman turning in his chair back to face his desk across from his partner.

"Yeah, I hope so too brother." Said Riviera.

"Now all we can do is wait to see what happens." Said Goodman.

"Are you going to the burial?" Asked Riviera.

"Can't. Jr., is coming over tonight for a week before school starts." Said Goodman puffing out a mouthful of air.

"Shit, good luck then brother," Said Riviera laughing.

"Yeah I'll need it said Goodman looking at a folder on his desk.

"Well, I'm going to head out. Catch you later, huh?" Riviera said standing.

"O.k. man, See ya." Goodman said, not looking up.

After an hour Goodman left his desk and left. The day was nice and clear he thought as he approached his vintage '67 5.0. He got in and let the top down, cranked the car and it roared to life. It idled for a bit and he thought about how time has really changed. Things were different now, these punk kids don't have any self respect or dignity. No consideration for nobody at all and have no understanding. Everything had to end in a shooting and not with just a little fist fight. Kids these days would rather take a chance with a bullet hole to the chest than a busted lip or nose. 'Fucking cowards' he thought. He pushed his thoughts away and turned his car stereo dial up and Journey started blaring from his car speakers. It made him feel better and he put the car in gear. It purred beautifully before he backed out of his parking spot, shifted gears, and peeled away leaving exhaust smoke lingering in the wind.

Chapter 22

"Cris, Cris, wake up." Whispered Reneé right in my ear and even bit it a little. We had fucked for a couple of hours straight nonstop. I was tired. Here I was trying to take a nap and regain my energy, but baby wasn't trying to hear it.

"Cris wake up" she says louder and crawls on top of me naked. Her hair cascaded over me, it smelled good with shampoo. Her big tits fell soft on me.

"You trying to kill me girl?" I say with my eyes closed. I wrap my arms around her.

"Ha ha!" she giggled.

"What time is it babe?" I ask.

"Three thirty." she says, kissing my neck.

"Morning?" I ask and she laughs.

"Boy! No. Afternoon." She tells me and laughs. My dick started to bulge up again and she felt it and smiled.

"Can't get enough?" She asked teasingly.

How can I, especially with you on top of me." I tell her. She giggled.

"Baby, you're going to tell me what happened?" She asked me seriously. I haven't had the chance to tell Reneé anything yet, we've been too busy with each other.

"Shit." I just say and rub sleep off my face and Reneé rolls off of me and lays next to me with one hand propping her head up and I turn to my side and do the same. I took in a deep breath and let it out.

"Where do you want me to start?" I ask her.

"What happened at Lance's burial?" She asked.

I know I said that us niggas tell our bitches too much after we got some pussy and I stand by that, but Reneé wasn't just any bitch I'm fucking. She is my girl, the woman I'm in love with and trust. It's different. She'll have my back regardless of the situation. Real talk. So I tell her all of it, from getting into it with my mom up until I got to Ro's crib. I left out going to see Rico cause that really wasn't that important. Just cause she was my girl I didn't feel like stressing her with any of that. I haven't even decided on anything yet anyways, so why talk about it. I'll cross that bridge when I get to it.

"I got a confession to make" She tells me.

"Say ten hail Mary's and five our father's and you are forgiven my daughter." I tell her being goofy.

"Ew, stop. That sounds weird." She says and laughs at me with a soft punch to my chest. "You're stupid babe." She tells me and pushes my face with her little hand.

"Girl, don't put your hand on my face. I don't know where its been?" I say to her. She reaches down and grabs my dick.

"Ow! o.k., o.k." I say flinching. "Keep playing with me." She says and goes back to being serious. "I called your mom while you were asleep." She says with a guilty face. I expected it so I wasn't surprised when she told me. And I wasn't mad at her.

"Yeah, I've been meaning to call her." I tell her feeling bad.

"She was crying when I last spoke to her. She told me to keep you safe. She loves you babe and she's your mom. You should be thankful that you still have her." Reneé said and tears started to form in her eyes.

Reneé 's mom died giving birth to her third child and they both didn't make it., so I felt where she was coming from. It's hard to have to lose a parent at a really young age. I can kinda relate in a way, but at least both of my parents are still alive. Thank God. I wipe the small tear off the corner of her eye. The tear wasn't for her mom, it was so long ago. I knew the tear was for me. I really didn't deserve this girl. Her heart was so big and she always put everybody else who she loved and cared about first. She was unselfish and loyal. If only all women were the same, but in all honesty us men are the ones that fuck it up and make women change and become mean selfish bitches. We always seem to fuck up a good thing, or try to fix what don't need fixing. Just need some understanding.

"I'll call her in a lil bit after I finish my meal right in front of me first." I say and go to reach for Reneé .

"You're going to call your mom first." She stops me and puts her cell in my face. "While you do that I'll go make us something to eat." She tells me and gets out of bed quick before I stop her.

"Really? So you gonna do me like that?" I ask her and watch her get dressed to go.

"You'll be o.k. you'll have me for dessert." She laughs and winks at me and struts away.

God she looks good from behind. I sigh and lay back down and grab her cell. Turn it on and a picture of us both pops up as her screen saver. I just smile.

I dial the house number by memory and put the phone to my ear and listen to it ring. It rang only once before my mom answered.

"Cris?" She sounded excited. She knew it was me calling. Us men will never understand a mother's intuition and her connection to her child. So strong, that even with the umbilical cord cut off that bond is still there no matter what.

"Hey lady." I called her that ever since I can remember. It was all love.

"Hey Cris come home please." She pleaded with me.

I couldn't stay mad at my mom. She was my real ride or die.

"Dear Momma"

By 2-Pac

Chapter 23

Monday Morning-Homicide Headquarters Downtown.

"So how did the funeral go buddy?" Asked Det. Goodman freshly shaven and looking a bit better.

"Not a way I would have liked to spend my Saturday. So much pain and sorrow." Said Riviera.

"Trust me I've been to plenty of them to know how you feel. It's part of the job and as bad as this may sound you'll get used to it. It's like you'll become numb to them, but it'll push you to continue to do your best and catch the people responsible for it all." Goodman explains.

"I know but she was so young and still had her life ahead of her and it came to a sudden stop 'cause of somebody being reckless." Riviera says and shakes his head.

"I get it buddy, that's why we do what we do. So what did you find out?" Asked Goodman trying to push the focus to the job at hand and leave the sad place alone.

"Things were very interesting, it got me nervous to be honest." Riviera said.

"Why's that?" Goodman asked puzzled.

"Well for starters it didn't look like a normal funeral that you would normally see with children." Explains Riviera.

"How you mean?" Still trying to figure out what his partner meant.

"It's liked it was a fellow gang member was being buried instead of an 8 year old little girl. I mean there were red bandanas everywhere, and the looks I got made me very uncomfortable, like it was my fault she died." Said Riviera.

"Wow" Said Goodman.

"I know right, I thought I was going to be part of a shootout myself glad I made it out alive, thank God." Said Riviera.

"Yeah, thank God." Said Goodman sarcastically.

"Ha, ha. I should've made you go with me." Riviera said following his partners humor.

"Sorry, had things to do. Plus, you're lead Detective in this anyway." Stated Goodman.

"How did it go? Asked Riviera changing the subject real quick.

"Great! Caught an Astros game and worked on the 5.0. a bit. I dropped him off with his friends at Six Flags this morning, so I'm covered for a while." Said Goodman smiling.

"Lucky you. But back to the funeral. I don't think this is close to being over." Said Riviera.

'Yeah, I was thinking about that as well. I feel like things are going to start to get very interesting real quick and we're not going to be able to stop it." Said Goodman.

"I feel the same way partner. I saw the looks on them guy's faces, they're out for revenge and anybody who's anybody is a potential target for them right now." Stated Riviera.

"And there isn't enough boots on the street to stop it." Finished Goodman.

"Nope, there isn't. So what do we do?" Asks Riviera.

"Keep our ears to the street and stay alert and ready for anything. Times like these we can't put our guards down." Said Goodman.

"What about your contact at the news station, are they going to run the story again?" Asked Goodman.

"Yeah, at 6pm. It'll be better 'cause more people are home by those hours. Have a better chance then, hopefully." Said Riviera.

"Sounds good. Our window is closing and we need to arrest somebody before we have too many homicides happening." Goodman said and sighed.

"Roger that." Riviera said.

"We need to catch a break and soon." Said Goodman and sighed.

Chapter 24

"Oh shit, give me that dick baby. Fuck!" Moaned and screamed Evelyn as Damion pounded away at her luscious big round dark brown booty.

"Uh, uh, uh! Oh daddy! Don't stop, don't stop! Uhm." She cried in pleasure.

Damion grabbed her by the hair and really started to dig inside of her guts, all you heard was skin and balls smacking. Not even the noise of their sexual pleasures could drown it out.

"I'm coming papi! I'm all on your dick. Cojamé mas duro! Mé vengo!" Evelyn screamed in Spanish.

Damion loved it when she talked that Spanish shit. It made him put in on her more and more.

"Here I come baby. I'ma bust a nut! Ah!" Damion hollered as he pulled his dick out of Evelyn and busted all on her ass.

"Shit mami! Got damn that pussy's fucking good. Uh." Damion said as he storke his dick and got all his cum out and onto Evelyn's ass cheeks.

"You like it papi?" She asked wiggling her ass side to side.

"Uh huh. Girl, I can't believe you pushed 5 kids out that pussy. It's still tight as fuck."

Damion said and then started putting his pants back on. He and Evelyn met at a night club. Evelyn's baby daddy was locked up and doing 20 years in the pen. Crazy thing about it is he only has to do 5 years before being able to see parole. Fucking hoe couldn't hold her man down for that long. Damion knew not to try to cuff the bitch no matter how good the pussy was. To make matters worse was that she had another sugar daddy that took care of her and paid her bills. Bitches ain't shit. Damion didn't mind breaking her off tho, it was all part of the hustle and he respected the hustle.

"Am I going to see you soon papi?" Evelyn said.

"I'll hit you up ma'.Here." He tells her and hands her a few bills. Right then her phone rings and she grabs it and looks at the screen. She puts her fingers to her mouth so that Damion don't say shit. He knew it meant it was her baby daddy.

"Hey babe, I was just thinking about you my love." She said answering the phone. Damion left without saying goodbye and got into his red Acura Integra sitting on black racing rims. He loved his car like he loved his women. Fast. He cranks it on and the exhaust system hums to life, puts it in first and takes off. The rice rocket shot forward quickly and he wasn't shy to put his foot down on the peddle. Ten minutes later he was turning on DeSoto St. and pulling up to B-Mo's trap house. He finds a parking spot and parks. He saw some of his homie's outside holding the block down and serving dope fiends.

"What's Poppin Damu!" Damion hollers at his homie Ra-Ra

"What it is dawg." Ra-Ra answers in return and they lock up B's.

"Chillin'. What's it looking like out here?" Asked Damion referring to the traffic.

"It's still early, but they coming." Said Ra-Ra. Damion sold crack, coke, weed, xanax, whatever B-Mo got a plug on they sold it and bought everything from guns to cars and clothes.

"B-Mo around?" Asked Damion.

"He inside." Answered Ra-Ra. Damion headed that way to to go holler at B-Mo. He really didn't want to see B-Mo right now, but he was summoned. He'd been up for 2 days straight sniffing coke and he was just coming off of it. His conscious was killing him 'cause of what happened to Regina. But he kept telling himself that it was an accident. But he knew that B-Mo wasn't trying to hear it for shit. But he was sure that B-Mo couldn't possibly find out that it was him that's responsible for his sisters death. It was impossible!

"What's poppin'?" Damion says going into the apartment and walking to the little table B-Mo and some other homies were at playing some dominos. B-Mo had a 40 oz. next to him and weed smoke was everywhere.

"What's da deal?" B-Mo says in return and they lock B's as well.

"Not shit. Wassup? You said you needed to see me." Said Damion.

"Yeah, we got a couple of lil niggas that are trying to get put down with the set." B-Mo said.

"Yeah? That's wassup! Where they at? Let's do the damn thing." Damion said enthusiastically. He loved shit like this.

"We'll get to that, but I gotta holla at'cha first. I got something on my mind." B-Mo said slurring a lil. He was obviously drunk. Ever since he lost his sister B-Mo hasn't been the same. Which was understandable. He wasn't the same dude, his attitude was more aggressive and his demeanor was on another level. Re-Re was his life. He loved his sister to the fullest. With their father locked up, he felt it was his responsibility to take care of his mother and sister. He felt guilty that he wasn't there to protect her and it was eating him up inside.

"So wassup?" Asked Damion. B-Mo got up and stumbled a little bit.

"Follow me. Hey Lil D, play my hand. I'll be back."

B-Mo said and walked to another room. B-Mo goes into another room and starts busting some weed down to smoke.

"My T-Jones got a phone call from the investigator with the ballistic report. B-Mo said. Damion's heart skipped a beat.

"What they say?" Damion's asked nervously. "They told my mom that Re-Re was shot and killed by a .357 bullet." B-Mo said and stopped busting the weed and just looked at it.

"Damion, don't you got a .357?" B-Mo asked and when he turned to look at Damion he had a sinister look in his eyes. It brought chills to Damion, instantly.

"Yeah, I did. I sold it a while back after we hit that house up where we got them guns, remember?" Damion came up with quick. It was actually part true. They did hit a lick a few months ago and came up on some money, guns, and drugs. Damion kept a couple of guns for himself as a matter of fact. But he never could bring himself to sell his pride and joy .357 glock SIG seur. They weren't very common in the street and he loved how it roared every time he busted it. Little Regina wasn't the only victim to the .357, even with Damion putting a body on it before, he still carried it. Maybe now it was time to get rid of it once and for all.

"Who did you sell it to?" Asked B-Mo curious.

"I sold it to my Mexican bitch Reynalda's cousin Big John." Damion said and lifted his shirt and exposed a 40 glock.

"See" said Damion. B-Mo relaxed some and let some air out of his mouth. He knew Big John, a Mexican cat out of Spring Branch. He also controlled the dope game in his hood and had a crew called. "J.Q.A." (Juntos, Queridos, Assesinos.

"Alright bro, my fault if I came at you sideways. I'm just trying to eliminate as much as possible. "Re-Re was my sister and I won't rest until I find the motherfucker who killed her." B-Mo said and a tear fell out of his eye.

"I'm with you Damu. To the end dawg." Assured Damion.

"Now let's take care of these lil homies and put em down fa sho." Said B-Mo getting up.

"Swoop!" Hollered Damion and the call was repeated throughout the spot. It was somebody's lucky day to bind themselves to a color for the rest of their lives. No do over's, no time outs, no hold ups. This was it, only way out was in a box buried in the ground 6 ft deep.

Chapter 25

I was cleaning my pistol and jamming to some music. It was like therapy to me when I cleaned my gun. Even though I haven't had to bust it yet. I wanted to make sure it didn't fail me when I did. I target practiced with it sometimes, but that was it. I wasn't a trigger happy type of dude, like some of my homies were. If I had to bust my gun on somebody I was going to make sure I hit and not miss. All I had was 5 shots so I had to make them count. As I cleaned my baby I was thinking about Rico's offer and was really considering on taking it. I just couldn't make up my mind.

Rico understood why I didn't jump onto his offer. He knew I wasn't a crash dummy. Even he said he saw me as a potential leader and respected my gangster.

Bruce Lee once said "The most dangerous person is the one who listens, thinks, and observes."

I believed that to the fullest and did just as he said. "Damn, I need a come up. Bad!" I said to myself. Just then my house phone rang and I answered it.

"Yo." I said to the receiver.

"Locs, what's crackin cuzzo?" My homie Kevin said. Me and Kevin have known each other for a while. Good nigga, but scary as fuck.

"Wassup." I say wondering what he wanted.

"Cuzzo, I need to holla atcha. Can I come by? I'll blow one with you." Kevin said and got my attention.

"Shit alright. In how long will you be here?" I asked.

"Bout ten minutes cuzzo, I'm getting cigars right now." He said. Damn, this nigga already had it on his mind didn't he.

"Alright, bet. Come through." I say.

"Say, I got my chick with me. That cool?" It didn't sound like a question to me.

"I guess you're already close by. Fuck it. But if Reneé pulls up out of no where I better not get shit from her." I tell him.

"Nah cuzz, I got you. He assures me.

"Alright. Duece!" I say and hang up.

I wrapped it up on cleaning my gun and put my shit away. Just when I slid it under my mattress there was a knock at my door.

(Knock Knock)

My sister Lorena opened my door. When I came back me and my mom had a talk. We said our sorry's, hugged, she kissed me and made dinner. She knew how to win my heart, through my stomach.

"Sup Sissy?" I say to my beautiful sister.

"Hey Cris, you busy?" She asked.

"Nah, not really." I said, acting like I was fixing my bed. She wasn't dumb.

"Cris, I want to go to the movies with my friends." She tells me.

"O.K., you tell mommy?" I ask her.

"Yes. But." She elaborated.

"Let me guess, you need some money? Right? I say to her and she nods her head. I reach into my pocket and shake my head at the same time. "Hol up, why an I giving you money. You was just at dad's this past weekend." I tell her.

"But Cris, I'm saving my money to buy something at the mall. I need movie money. She explained. By the time I pull my money clip out and peel off two twenties she already had her hand out.

"Thanks Cris!" She tells me, gives me a kiss and hug and turns to run. Then stops.

"I'm glad you're back. Mommy and I missed you. Don't run away again." She scolded me. I just smile at her. Then there was a knock at the door.

"Go, get out of here." I tell her.

"Who's that?" She asked being nosy.

"None of your business." I tell her and lead her out the door, close it and lock it. I lived in the back of the house and before my dad got caught up he had converted this room into an office. He smoked cigars so he had to be able to let the smoke out somehow 'cause my mom didn't want the house stinking up. Now it was my room and I was able to go and come without having to go through the front.

"Wassup?" I say answering the door. I see Kevin but what really got my attention was the chick standing next to him. When I say this girl was fine, I mean fine! She reminded me of the porn star Pinky that I was so infatuated with. Only she was Latino.

"Sup Cuzzin." Said Kevin smiling.

"Come in." I said stepping to the side and letting them pass. Ol' girl has ass like Bam! They both sit on the edge of my soft bed and I leaned back in my computer chair.

"Who's this?" I ask Kevin.

"This my girl Dulcé" Kevin introduces.

"Holá" She says in Spanish.

"¿Qué tal mami, como esta?" I ask her in return and hit her with my Spanish.

"Bién" She says and smiles.

"So what's up? You got some rillos?" I ask so we can smoke.

"Yeah here." He says and hands me the box of cigars.

"I got it papi." Says Dulcé and gets up and so do I so she can sit on my chair. I go sit on my bean bag to relax. When Dulcé sits down I couldn't stop myself from looking at her thick thighs and she was wearing a mini skirt. It rose up a lot and I was able to catch a glimpse of her shaved area She didn't have any panties! Oh. Em. Gee. She saw me looking and she just smiled.

"So what's up Kev?" I asked my homie and trying to concentrate.

"I got a lick for you." He tells me. I finally take my eyes off of Dulcé's sugar pot and look at Kevin.

"What you mean?" I asked.

"Okay. Dulcé is an escort/stripper. But after we met she decided that she didn't want to do that anymore." Kevin said. I can't tell I thought to myself. She opened her legs more all of a sudden when I looked back at her.

"So what's the lick?" I ask. This time Dulcé spoke.

"I got a homegirl that does what I do and is fucking this guy that owns his own construction company." She said and rolling at the same time.

"They meet up all the time and she even told me that sometimes he carry's up to $10,000. Maybe more." She continued.

"O.k." I say waiting for her to continue.

"He's got a safe and keeps it all there. She told me he' got a lot of gold too." Dulcé says.

"So what. Ya'll want to rob him?" I ask.

"No. We want you to rob him." Said Kevin.

"And what do I get?" I asked.

"$2,000 for every $10,000, plus half the gold." Kevin says.

"So what? I'm supposed to do all the work and only get 2g's? What ya'll going to be doing?" I ask.

"We'll be at a near by hotel waiting." Kevin said.

"Fuck that!" I say shaking my head.

"Well, what would you want?" Asked Dulcé, like she was offering herself. I thought about it for a bit.

"Give me 3g's and half the jewels." I tell him. Kevin and Dulcé look at each other and she nods. So she's the boss huh?

"O.k." Says Kevin.

"Alright. Find out when and where and let me know something." I say and relax a little.

"We got a plan." Kevin says all happy and shit. Rookie. We smoke some weed and chill. How the fuck did this nigga get such a fine ass bitch in the first place?! "

Creepin On A Come Up"

By Bone Thugs

Chapter 26

"Mom!" I yelled going to the living room.

"I'm in the kitchen mijo." She calls back to me.

After we chopped it up and smoked two blunts. Kevin and his fine ass bitch took off. That nigga got lucky with Dulcé and her slutty ass self. Who am I kidding, I hit dice when Reneé made me her man, but us niggas all got a lil bit of dog in us and can't resist ourselves. Even when we got a good girl by our side that loves us to the fullest we end up fucking shit up by fucking with a slut bucket. But ain't nothing wrong with just looking is there?

"Damn, it smells good in here lady, what you cooking?" I ask giving my mom a kiss on the cheek.

"Arros con leché" She said. She knew we loved that shit.

"Bet!" Hey mom, you going anywhere anytime soon?" I ask.

"No, why?" She asks looking at me.

"I need the Explorer, I gotta go to Henry's real quick and come back." Me and Ro stayed in the same neighborhood and just lived a few streets apart.

"O.k. but it's low on gas so fill it up for me so I don't have to do it. Grab some money from my purse." She tells me.

"Alright" I say, turned to leave when she called me again.

"Cristino!" She said.

"Yeah mom."

She called me with her finger and when I got close enough she grabbed my face by my cheeks.

"Be careful mijo. I can't stand the thought that I will lose you like the men I loved before. Oyistes?" She tells me.

"Yeah mom. You're trippin lady, you ain't going to lose me." I assure her.

She gives me a kiss on the mouth and pushes my face away.

"Ugh. You smell of mota. Go! Get out of here." She says.

"Love you mom. I'll be right back." I say and shoot out without going into her purse. I ain't no bum.

I get to Ro's banging the music loud. My dad owned his own car lot and had really nice cars to sell. So of course he gave my mom a good car every time something happened to it. Sometimes it was something simple, but out of spite she would take it back and pick something else out that she liked and made sure it was fully loaded. My mom still had my dad by the balls.

On the cool, I think they still sneak and see each other. Can't prove it, but I can tell when my mom comes back from being gone for a couple of hours happy as she was when he was home and heads straight to the shower. Cochinos.

I park the ride and hop out. I noticed Ro's mom's ride was gone. I should've called but his mom probably had her car and he's usually home. I knocked on the door and waited a minute before I saw a figure coming behind the foggy glass on the door. Once the figure got closer I was able to make out that it was Cookie. Damn, this bitch ain't got her own home?

Cookie opens the door and stood there in some very small booty shorts and skimpy tank top, with no bra. She didn't need one to be honest. and she was too young for implants so they were naturally nice and round. Just observing.

"Sup Cris." She said my name sensually.

"Hey, Ro here." I say stepping in without an invite. Mi casa, sú casa. Type shit.

"No. He took his mom to a Dr.'s appointment about ten minutes ago." She said shutting the door and locking it.

"Damn I needed to holla at that nigga. Tell him I came by and to get at me asap." I tell her going around her to leave in the small entrance way. She put her hand out and palm on the wall to stop me.

"Leaving so soon?" She asks me and getting close to me. I could smell her.

"Yeah, Ro's not here so why wouldn't I leave?" I tell her.

"Chill with me. I got a sweet rolled up and we can smoke it. Together." She said that last word with extra meaning.

"Naw ma, that won't be a good idea. Plus it wouldn't seem right." I tell her.

"Who cares about what it seems like?" She said, comes much more close and in an instant reaches for my dick and grabs it. Why did I have to be wearing basketball shorts? I ain't going to lie, it felt good and

113

my shit got hard instantly. She felt it too 'cause she smiled and come in for a kiss.!

"Yo ma, I can't do this." I say to her, pushing away.

"Nobody has to know. And I think you want to as well, as hard as your dick is." She says and strokes me more. Blood finally reaches my brain and started thinking again. I reach down and grab her hand and take it off me.

"Cookie, I'm with Reneé and you're with Ro. He's like a brother to me." I tell her while I tried to escape.

"So? You know how I feel about you and been wanting you Cris and don't lie baby." She said and grabbed one of her tits and squeezing it.

"You want this pussy too." She said licking her lips and rubbing herself.

"Nah ma' I love Reneé and I can't do that. Ro loves you too." I try to plead with her.

"If he loved me then he wouldn't allow me to fuck other dudes for money." She says. I'd almost felt sorry for her.

"It's o.k. to fuck guys that he wants me to fuck for money, but what about the guys I want to fuck? Like you Cris." She tells me and tries to grab my dick again. I stepped back this time and grab her wrist--tight.

"Look Cookie. You're a beautiful woman, but nobody can make you do what you don't want to do." I tell her pushing her hand away.

"And what about what I want to do?" She says and tries one more time to kiss me. This time I push her off of me so hard that she stumbles back and falls on her ass.

"Bitch! I told you no! You deaf or something?!" I scream at her.

"Fuck you nigga! I'm calling the cops on your ass!" She said loud. She must have seen the surprised look in my eyes 'cause she laughed.

"Oh what? You ain't think I watched the news motherfucker? I saw your photo on TV and guess what? If you would've just given me what I wanted." She said opening her legs and I could see some of her pussy meat through the side of her shorts.

"We would've been OK and I wouldn't have turned you in!" She said and laughed showing off her icy white teeth.

"Bitch you got me fucked up hoe!" I say and pull my gun out to pop her bitch ass.

"Go ahead! Shoot me nigga! That way they can get you for two murders!" She says and laughs.

"You ain't worth it bitch." I say tucking my pistol back in my pocket. I step over her to go before I did something that would get me fucked off later.

"Your loss baby." She says and was still laughing when I shut the door behind me. Got in my mom's Explorer and peeled out up out of there.

Chapter 27

<u>Ten Minutes Later</u>

"We got him!" Riviera slams his desk phone down. Goodman came around the corner from using the restroom and caught just that part.

"What's up?" Asked Goodman.

"We got him! We got the sonofabitch!" Exclaimed Riviera excited.

"Got who? What are you talking about?" Asked Goodman still confused.

"The kid from the Regina Morris shooting. Somebody just called in and gave me a name." He said grabbing his badge and gun out from his desk drawer.

"So what do you got?" Asked Goodman.

"A name and address." Said Riviera.

"Hold on let's check the computer real fast and see what we find out before we do anything. Don't get too excited partner." Goodman said and sat down at his desk and moved the mouse around two get the screen saver off.

"What's the name?" He asked Riviera who was now standing behind his partner.

"Cristino Segovia." Riviera read from a notebook.

"And the address?" Asked Goodman.

"10754 Corona Ln." Riviera read out.

"Bingo." Said Goodman.

"Well I'll be damned." Said Goodman.

"What is it?" Asked Riviera.

"This address is way across town in Alief." Said Goodman.

"Alief? What the hell was he doing in the other side of town?" Wondered Riviera.

"That's a good question that we'll have to ask him ourselves." Said Goodman.

"So does it say anything on him?" Asked Riviera.

"Yeah hold on let me check." Goodman said, typing away.

"OK, here we go." Goodman said. "Cristino Segovia, 16 years old. Born 1987 of September 23rd. Mother's name is Anna Segovia Bonilla." Said Goodman.

"Is that it?" Asked Riviera anxious.

"Hold your horses pal. Let me see if he's got a record." Typed away Goodman.

"Here we go." Goodman said pulling something up.

"He's been taken to Makawa Youth Detention Center for fighting in school. Nothing serious enough to get in real trouble. Mommy always got him out." Said Goodman.

"Here goes something, there's his picture and thumbprints." Goodman said opening the image box and a picture appeared.

"That's him, that's the kid!" Screamed Riviera.

"Let's see. Yep he's a gang member after all. That explains all the blue. Hmm. 'Insane Gangsta Crip! I've never heard of that gang before around here." Said Goodman puzzled.

"It's not from around here, they're based out of Austin, but it is an original set out of California." Said Riviera.

Goodman just looked at him with surprise.

"What? I grew up in the hood what do you expect?" Riviera said defensively.

"Height 5'8" 220 lbs. Big boy." Exclaimed Goodman.

"So, what now?" Asked Riviera standing up straight.

"We take what we got, take it to a judge and get a warrant." Said Goodman as a matter of factly.

"Well what are we waiting for partner? This is our break we've been waiting for. Let's go!" Said Riviera excited.

"Alright partner. You lead, it's your case." Goodman said getting up and off they went to see a judge.

Chapter 28

I screech to a halt in the driveway when I pull up to my crib, jump out and go inside straight to my room. I go to my closet and pull out my big duffle bag that I used to pack clothes in whenever I would go spend some time at my dad's. Now I packed it to leave for a bit. If Cookie was as crazy as she sounded and was for real about calling the laws on me then I had to prepare for the worst.

As I load my bag up my mom came into my room. Damn I didn't want to face her right now.

"Cris? What are you doing? What's going on?" She asked me worried. I stopped when I heard my name and looked at her. One thing I've learned is that you don't lie to your mom when you was in trouble. Especially when they was going to be the only one that's really going to be there for you at the end of whatever you're going thru. My mom always told me that it was best for me to be honest with her no matter what I did 'cause she couldn't defend me if I lied to her and made her look stupid.

"Mom, I got to go." I simply said.

"Go? Go where? What's going on Cristino?" She asked crossing her arms. She had no clue of what happened that day after I left from Lance's funeral. I felt it was going to blow over and I would be good. Bitch ass McDonald's.

"Mom I got to tell you something." I said and proceeded to tell her every single detail. Except about the fact that I had a gun, I didn't want to unload all that on her at one time. By the time I finished telling her what happened she was sitting on my bed.

"But you didn't do anything mijo. So why are they looking for you?" She asked.

"Cause I'm the only person that they say was there. Nobody saw the dude who was actually shooting. And that neighbor said she saw me hiding." I tell her.

"Dios mio." My mom said. "But they don't know who you are or they would have been here by now right?" She asked. Mom is super down.

Then I continued to tell her about what just happened with Cookie at Ro's crib.

"¡Esa pinche' perra sucia maldita! I knew I didn't like her for a good reason." My mom said pissed.

"So what's your plan mijo?" Asked my mom.

"Well if she did call the cops then they'll be here real soon. So I figured I'd hide at Reneé 's or Randy's." I tell her. Randy was my big homie who put me down with the set a year after he came to Houston from Austin Texas.

"OK, but how will we keep in touch? She asked. The lady was ride or die for real.

"I'ma be at Reneé 's, but if anything I'll tell Ro to let you know if anything changes. Okay?" I tell her and she starts to cry.

"Mom don't cry. Everything's going to be o.k. I promise. I really didn't do anything, but the laws just need to arrest anybody just so that they can look good! They don't care if you're really innocent." I tell her and she understands how the system works.

She grabs my hand, kisses it and pulls me in for hug and kiss.

I'm going to kick Reneé's ass 'cause she didn't tell me shit before." She says and it makes me laugh.

"Let me finish packing and you can drop me off at her house. I got to move fast mom. If I need anything else I'll have to call you for it, but be careful what you say on the phone. K?" I tell her and looking at her eyes.

"O.k. Hurry up before Lorena comes back from the movies and sees you leave. She tells me and goes.

Didn't everybody wish they had a momma like me?

"Amor De Madre"

By Aventura

Chapter 29

Tuesday-6:15a.m.

"OK, gentleman, can I have your undivided attention, please? Thank you. Gather around," Said Goodman, directing the men in gear. All of them had bulletproof vests on and were dressed in black; some even had their faces painted black.

"All right. I won't take long with this speech. This is our suspect. Take a good look at him." Goodman said, passing a photo around.

"He is suspected to be armed and dangerous, so approach with caution and haste," He continued.

"We are to execute this warrant as quickly and efficiently as possible. We want to avoid any confrontation and minimize the threat. There will be non-hostiles occupying the residence—a mother and child. But still be on alert," Said Goodman.

"I want to thank every one of you gentleman for volunteering for this mission. Our goal is to take any threat to our society off the streets and make it safe for our children." Goodman spoke with purpose.

"God bless us, and may He look over us. Hoorah!" He yelled.

"Hoorah!" the men yelled in return. They all crowded into SUV's and a van that read S.W.A.T. and headed to 10754 Corona Ln. Once they arrived at their destination, they cut the lights and parked. They all got out and rushed around the house, but made no noise to arouse anybody sleeping. Once the location was secured, the signal was made for clear, and then they made noise.

(Bang! Bang! Bang!)

"Open up! HPD!" One guy said, not even a second later, the front door was knocked down.

(Bam Crash!)

They flooded into the house, flashlights illuminating every direction. Then a woman was spotted coming out of a hallway in her robe.

"Freeze!" One man barked, and all flashlights were on her in an instant.

"Hold fire! It's the mother," One yelled. Then another figure appeared next to the mother.

"Hold fire! It's a child," Another guy barked. Both were escorted outside safely.

"What's going on?" Asked the woman/

"Step right over here, ma'am please!" Ordered Goodman.

"Continue!" Goodman barked as he led the woman and child out.

"What is going on here?" Demanded the woman.

"Ms. Segovia, we are looking for your son, Cristino Segovia. Here's the warrant." He said, handing her a copy of it. She instantly started to read it.

"I don't know! He hasn't been home in days. I caught him smoking that God-awful marijuana and told him he had to stop or leave. I wouldn't tolerate that in front of my daughter," She lied so well. Lorena was crying, and the woman had her arms wrapped around her, trying to protect her from what was going on.

"What do you want with my son?" Asked the lady.

"Your son was seen at an apartment complex where a little girl, your daughter's age was shot and killed," Goodman said.

"So, just because he was seen there, all this is happening?" Asked the woman.

"Ma'am, we're trying to get to the bottom of all this!" Said Riviera. Goodman raised a hand to stop him from going off. Good cop, bad cop.

"Ms. Segovia , something happened, and your son knows what it was that caused someone to die. Now, I'm sure that if your daughter were that same girl you would want answers as well, wouldn't you?" Said Goodman.

"Leave my daughter out of this! I know how the system works, señor."

The woman snarled and continued. "Instead of innocent 'til proven guilty, it's guilty 'til proven innocent." She said with anger.

"Now hold on senora!" Riviera cut in.

"We're just trying to do our jobs here and solve a case." Said Riviera.

"Well my son isn't here so your job is done for right now. So I'd appreciate ya'll leave my property. Now!" She said loudly.

The two detectives stared at the lady a second then Goodman spoke. "Let's wrap it up. It's a bust. Let's move out." He ordered and everybody moved in unison. He stayed back a little and reached into a vest pocket and came out with a card.

I'm only trying to help your son. Honestly. Please call me if you have any contact with him. He said handing her the card.

"If you really want to help then stay and fix my door." She said and snatched the card. Goodman just smiled and left. Once out of earshot Lorena spoke for the first time.

"How did I do mommy?" She asked.!"

"You did good baby. Come on, let's go inside." She said and led her daughter inside.

"So what do you think? Asked Riviera to Goodman.

"She knows where he's at. She doesn't seem like the type of person to sell out her child. Let's keep an eye on her for mean while." Goodman said.

"Roger that." Riviera said using his cell and put the car in drive.

"Reneé , the bacon is on the fryer for breakfast." Anna said on the phone in her room.

"OK. You good?" Asked Reneé .

"Yeah fine. My love," Anna said and hung up.

125

Chapter 30

9:45am.

Cereal was popping in a bowl of milk and Damion was just going to take first big bite when the bell rang at his door.

"Fuck." He said and spooned a mouthful and got up with the bowl to see who was at his door disturbing his breakfast.

"What's poppin' Damu!?" Said Lil Trip when Damion opened his door.

"Goddamn lil nigga what happened to you?" Asked Damion and moving out the way to let his lil homie in. Damion could see Trip had a busted lip.

"I got into a squabble with some crab at the park yesterday." Said Trip with pride.

"Yeah? And did you win?" Asked Damion closing the door and spooning more cereal into his mouth.

"Pshh. What you think?" Said offended Trip.

"Aight my bad killer." Said Damion laughing and dropping his dishes in the sink.

Lil Trip was 13 years old and had just got put down with the set a few days ago. Damion liked the little dude and saw potential in him and took him under his wing. They've been rockin' out together ever since.

"So what happened?" Asked Damion coming back and crashed on the couch.

"I was walking out to the corner store and I had my flag out hangin' and this crab ass nigga started set trippin' and talkin' shit." He explained.

"And then?" Asked Damion sparking a blunt up.

"He gets to stackin' on me and I stacked back like you showed me and then he run up on me and we started fighting." Trip finished.

"That's why I got you under me lil homie, you ain't no bitch or scary. You did right dawg." Said Damion passing Trip the lit blunt.

"Already big homie." Said Trip taking the blunt and hitting it. Just then Damion had an idea.

"Wait right here lil homie. I'll be back." Damion said and went to his room. He reached into his nightstand next to his bed and pulled out the .357. He contemplated the idea a bit, but finally decided it was best. It was now officially a throw away and couldn't keep it.

"Better not keep it." He said to himself and then pulled out a wad of cash and peeled off a couple of bills and grabbed an ounce of weed also and went back to the living room.

"Here." He said and dropped the bud in Trip's lap as he sat back down. Damion sat right next to Trip and relaxed on the sofa.

"What's this?" Asked Trip.

"What you think dummy?" Said Damion.

"I mean what's it for?" Asked Trip again.

"That's an ounce you can break down and sell sweets for $5.00 a pop." Damion explains to Trip. "You should make about $65.00 all together. Bring me back $30.00 and I'll get you another one." Said Damion smoking his blunt.

"Preciate it big homie!." Says Trip eyeballing the bag and playing with the nuggets in it.

"Here goes two bills. Get you some jay's and clothes. You can't keep looking like a bum homie." Damion said and before Trip could say anything else he passed him his last gift. Trips eyeballs went wide. "Here, that's yours. You're going to need protection out here. I ain't always gonna be around and one day a fight won't end right there." Damion said and Trip grabbed the pistol.

"Now be careful homie. It ain't a toy to play with so watch out. Keep it on safety." Damion said as Trip watched how to cock it, empty it and drop the magazine, and reload it.

Lil Trip just watched in amazement as Damion demonstrated. He made it look so easy and cool.

"You got it?" Asked Damion.

The kid just nodded. It's crazy how the young mind works. It's like a sponge that absorbs all it sees and records it forever.

"Remember. If anybody asks you, you got it from a dope fiend and not from me. You got it?" Asked Damion sternly.

"Fásho big homie." Said Lil Trip and went back to looking at his new gun.

"Shorty Wanna Be A Thug" By: 2 Pac

Chapter 31

I couldn't sleep after my mom called Reneé 's cell this morning. Me and her had already come up with a plan and what code words we were going to use. Actually she came up with the code words. I made fun of her for it and she told me that her and my tia Lily used to do the same when my mom had to let her sister know it was safe to come in thru the window after sneaking out.Not even having sex with my girl could put me to sleep, that's how much I had on my mind.

(Ring Ring)

Reneé 's phone was ringing and I grabbed it and answered it, it was Ro calling. I ain't spoke to him after the whole Cookie issue.

"Sup Cuzz." I said answering.

"Goddamn my nigga why you put yo hands on my bitch?!" Ro says mad.

"Hold up my nigga. First of all I pushed the bitch off me 'cause she was trippin'. And second." I started to say when I heard Ro laughing.

"Ha ha! Gotcha my nigga." Said Ro fucking with me.

"You play too much nigga. Say cuzz. That bitch came onto me and grabbed my shit." I tell Ro, making sure Reneé didn't hear me.

"Man, that hoe was crying talking about you slapped her and shit 'cause she ain't let you fuck." Ro said.

"Man cuzz, that bitch lying bro on my momma! You know I don't get down like that my nigga!" I almost had to check my voice 'cause Reneé was in the shower and I didn't tell her about Cookie to avoid more problems.

"Man nigga I already know what kind of bitch she is. After she told me that when I got home yesterday I kicked the bitch out." Ro said to me.

"Good. And the bitch actually called the laws on me Ro!" I told him.

"What? How you know?" Asked Ro.

"Cause she told me she was if I didn't fuck her and then the next morning they kicked my door in. They found out who I was 'cause of her and now I'm wanted for that lil girls murder." I tell him.

"What the fuck? I ain't know shit about that cuzz! For real." Ro said mad and this time it was real.

"Yeah bro. I've been here at Reneé 's since yesterday. My mom's on point about it all." I tell him.

"OK cool. No wonder you ain't been picking your house phone up." He said.

"I unplugged it before I left." I tell him in my normal voice now that it is safe to talk.

"So what? Just hit you up on here?" Asked Ro.

"Yeah but say I really need to holler at you. That's why I went to your place in the first place." I tell Ro.

"Alright then, I'ma pull up. You need anything?" Asked Ro.

"Bud." I simply said.

"Bet. See you in a bit." Ro said.

"Deuce." I said and hung up.

I dialed another number and the line rang. "Hello." answered Kevin.

"Kev. It's Locs. We still on for that issue?" I asked.

"Yeah, yeah!" He said excitedly. "I've been calling and calling your crib all day." Kevin said.

"Wassup?" I asked.

"It's on for Thursday night." Said Kevin."

"Alright, I'll call you tomorrow and chop it up." I say.

"Koo koo, Yo Locs" He said and I hung up. Whatever he wanted to talk about we can talk in person.

Chapter 32

<u>Later that day</u>

Ro finally got to Reneé 's and scooped me up. Me and baby were just chillin', but I was glad to finally get away from her. She was all emotional and shit. We was in the middle of fucking when all of a sudden she started crying. I didn't know what the fuck I did? I thought I hurt her, but I ain't working with nothing that big so I knew it wasn't anything to do with the sex. She admitted that she was scared to lose me, especially now that we started to get closer. She knew my lifestyle and was down, but she was still scared and she had every right to be. But I assured her that as long as we stay true to one another and love each other to the fullest that nobody can break that bonded chain between us. I knew Reneé was a strong woman and she loved me, but let's be honest. A woman can only put up with so much bullshit. But until the wheels fall off, am I right?

"So where we going?" Asked Ro when I jump in his ride.

"I gotta go check in with Randy. I gotta lace him up on what's going on real quick." I told Ro.

"He called you or what?" Asked Ro concerned.

"Nah, but I know it's something I got to do." I tell him.

"Yeah, you right. Here." Ro says and passes me a sack. I go to my pocket to pay him.

"Nah cuzz, that's on me. I know you need all you got right now."
Ro said driving.

"Preciate it cuzz." After I emptied my stash spot and counted my
savings I had a total of $4300, plus the few bills I kept on me at all times.
I was saving for my car, but now I was going to pay for a lawyer. I had to
see my dad soon too. I dreaded that part, but my mom told me she was
going to give him a heads up. I didn't like that idea.

"So what you gonna do cuzz?" Asked Ro.

"I don't know? I got to find a good lawyer and see how much
that is going to cost me." I say and sigh. We were 20 minutes from
Randy's so I twist a joint real quick and spark it.

"Yeah. So what did you need to holla at me about?" Ro reminded
me.

"Oh shit! I almost forgot." I exclaim and start telling him about
the lick Kevin proposed to me.

"So what you think?" I ask Ro for his honest opinion.

"When is it?" Asked Ro.

"Thursday night. " I got to get with Kev tomorrow." I tell him.

"Shit, if it's as easy as it sounds then cool, but we both know
shit's never easy." Ro said to me as I passed him the joint.

"I know." I said.

"Look, they think it's just you going, right? But they won't
expect me going with you." Says Ro getting my attention.

"What you saying Ro? You want to go with me? I'm only getting
3g's and some jewels." I said to him being honest.

"Nigga, I ain't doing it for the bread; I'm doing it to help you out 'cause I know you would do the same for me." Ro said and he was right.

"Man cuzz, you ain't got to do that, I got this!" I assured him.

"I know you do nigga, but I ain't asking you for your permission. I'm telling you." Ro said finally. His mind was made up.

I gave him my hand and we locked C's. It was understood. Enough said. We finally pull up to Randy's crib and park by the curb.

There were a few homies posted up outside already chillin. This was ground zero for us-- our thug mansion. The spot. We hop out and everybody was already looking at us to see who we were. The big homies been had this hood on lock, and you didn't come thru here unless you belonged, anybody else was suspect. Everybody else relaxed when they saw me and Ro walking up.

"Big Locs!" Hollered my homie Phillip when we got close.

"Sup cuzz!" I said and we all start locking c's up.

"Damn cuzz, you famous!" Said another homie named Robert.

"Naw Cuzz it ain't even like that." I tell him being humble.

"Shit Cuzz they trying to get your ass!" Say's Lil A laughing. Another homie.

"Man Cuzz, you lucky I fuck with you, 'cause that 10 g's reward sounded good." Spoke Robert playing and laughing.

"Ten g's?" I ask confused.

"Nigga you on the news and ain't been keeping up with it?" Said Randy behind me when he walked into the garage.

"Sup Cuzz! What's good big homie?" I tell Randy and we hug and lock c's. Randy met me when he was in the 11th grade and I was in the 8th grade. We was at a house party and we clicked ever since.

"Shit you tell me homie, what you got going on?" He asks sincerely.

"Man Cuzz." I just say to him and drop my head not knowing where to start."

"Come on let's go inside and talk." He puts his hand on my neck and grabs me for a hug like a brother.

"Ro, what's crackin' Cuzz!" He hollered before we went inside. "Sit down." Randy tells me so I sit on his couch. The place was a straight bachelor pad. Not a lot of furniture but loaded with game systems and a bad ass big TV with a kick ass surround system.

"What took you so long to come by Locs?" Asked Randy settling down.

"My bad cuzz." I didn't expect for it to escalate this far to be honest." I said to him feeling bad.

"So what the fuck happened?" He asked curious and reaches for a joint.

I told him what happened and to be honest I was tired of telling the same story over and over. I had to shorten it every time I had to tell it and just told the specifics.

"Damn cuzz, why didn't you pop that tomatohead's brains out?" Asked Randy taking a drag of the joint and passing it to me.

"Ro said the same thing, but by the time I got to a safe place, pulled my gun out and waited for him he had already stopped shooting and then took off." I tell him. Randy just shook his head.

"So what you gonna do now?" He asked me.

"I got to get a lawyer. They kicked my door in early this morning." I tell him and passed the joint back.

What I last said brought Randy to sit up and sit at the edge of the couch.

"Hol' up. They kicked your door in already? How they find you so fast? They ain't say shit about that on the news." He said and grabbed the remote and changed the channel.

I told him about Ro's bitch Cookie, and Randy dropped his head and shook it clearly upset.

"Fucking bitch!" He just said and then looked at me.

"He already said he'll take care of her." I answered 'cause I know what he was going to ask next.

"Good. So you got money to get a lawyer?" Randy asks.

"I got some. I don't know how much it's going to cost? But I got something lined up and hopefully it helps." I said without saying too much.

"Wait right here cuzz." He told me and left and comes back a minute later. "Here. Take this." He tells me and hands me a roll of cash.

"What's this?" I asked.

"It's money cuzz! What it look like nigga? You starting to worry me lil homie." He told me teasing me. I unrolled it and count it out. "It ain't much but it should help." Randy tells me.

I counted fifteen one hundred dollar bills.

"Naw cuzz, I really appreciate it, but I didn't come over here for a handout." I said to Randy.

"Man cuzzo it ain't like that. I know you didn't, but I do know you a real good lil nigga and I cut for you. You're my lil homie, what kind of big homie would I be if I didn't try to help?" Said Randy, passing back the joint.

"Thanks cuzz." I say stuffing the bills in my pocket.

"A piece of advice cuzz, get you a good lawyer. I know one that's good but expensive. If you want his number I'll get it for you." Randy said.

"Yeah that'd be good homie. 'Preciate it." I told Randy and he gets up to get the number for me.

"Now remember Locs, when they come for you and they will. Don't say a motherfucking thing. You don't want to incriminate yourself. Tell them that you plead the fifth and you want to talk to your lawyer. That's it! They'll try to play the good cop bad cop game so just stay quiet. Don't do their job for them, they are after one thing and one thing only and that's to find a reason to lock you up for a long time. The system don't give a fuck about you cuzz. Remember that!" Randy tells me with all seriousness.

"Aight cuzz. I hear you." I tell him.

If you're going to do dirt and be down with the shit then be ready to face the consequences and take your own lick I can't stand motherfuckers that swear to God they some down motherfuckers and ready to bust anybody who looks at them sideways. Then when they get popped they get to telling on other niggas that ain't got shit to do with why they got popped. You know what you signed up for so don't try to act all innocent like you didn't know what was going on. Just sayin'.

"Within Myself"

By: Trae and Z-Ro (screwed up)

Chapter 33

"So what's next partner?" Asked Riviera at his desk.

"Well we only got one more shot at going to the news station and giving them what we now got. Hopefully we'll be able to flush him out somehow." Said Goodman.

"But won't we risk him knowing that we know who he is and him make a run for it?" Asked Riviera concerned.

"Nobody really gets away from the law that easy partner. Eventually all of them get caught and brought to justice. It may be weeks, months. Hell maybe even years, but it's our job to not give up." Said Goodman proudly.

"He'll come back home soon, he's just a kid. He will run out of sources at some point. And he will start to get comfortable again and will make a mistake and I'm banking that when he does we'll be waiting on him with open arms." Goodman said and smiled.

"I hope you're right partner." Riviera said and got up to leave for the day.

"Where you going?" Asked Goodman with a surprised expression.

"I gotta go to that dinner party with Marie, remember? Her sister's getting married to her girlfriend Friday." Riviera said annoyed.

"That's today already? Time flies when having fun. I guess I'll have to call the news station and do the dirty work." Goodman said sarcastically.

"Thanks partner. I knew I could count on you." Riviera said patting his partner on the shoulder and headed out.

Goodman picked up the phone and called the news station. A movie with Junior sounded like a good idea tonight. Hell, the kid might get lucky and have pizza for dinner tonight as well.

Chapter 34

10:20 That Night.

"You saw that crab niggas face?" Asked B-Mo to Damion while they was outside posted up on the block.

"Yeah that's the nigga. It's crazy how they found out who he is before we did." Said Damion.

"I'm going to try to find out where he lives tomorrow and see if we can pay him a lil visit." B-Mo said with a snarl.

"Fa sho." Damion said and spotted Lil Trip walking his way.

"What's poppin' damu?" Trip said when he got closer.

"Yo, what's poppin' youngsta?" Said B-Mo.

"What up blood?" Damion said while they locked hands.

"I see your eye ain't as swollen." Noted Damion.

"Yeah I'm good." Said Trip.

"I heard 'bout you homie. That's wassup dawg, Don't let no crab nigga make it. Said B-Mo to Trip.

"Already." Trip answered back with pride.

"What you got for me?" Asked Damion.

Lil Trip lifted his big T-shirt in order to be able to reach into his pocket and in doing so he didn't realize how B-Mo was watching his every move. Neither did Damion. It was dark outside but the lights of the city didn't allow for stars to really shine at night.

B-Mo was able to notice Trips gun that was on his waist. Trip hands over a wad of cash to Damion and he counts it out oblivious to anything else.

"Say Lil homie that's a nice piece you got there. What is it?" Asked B-Mo just out of curiosity.

"Uhm......" Trip started to say and then cut his eyes to Damion who now stopped counting the money in his hand and looked back at Trip with wide eyes. B-Mo noticed Trips hesitation.

"I think it's a .357." Said Trip. After all his homie only said to not tell no one where he got it from. That was it. "Yeah, let me see it." B-Mo tells Trip.

Trip reaches for it not really knowing what was going on. But these were his big homies, so why not? Once B-Mo had it in his hand he automatically starts turning it in his hand and getting a feel on it. He cocked it halfway just to see if there was a bullet in it and when he saw it was clear he cocked it all the way and loaded the chamber. Clicked the safety on and handed it handle first back to Trip.

"Always keep one in the chamber lil homie." B-Mo said.

Damion finally took a breath. He was shitting bricks that very moment. If B-Mo only knew.

"Where you get it from dawg?" Continued B-Mo as Trip grabbed the pistol.

"I got it off a dope fiend for four rocks." Trip lied.

Damion started to sweat a little bit and the weather was pretty cool this time of year.

"That's a lot of power you packing right there. Don't fuck around and be careless lil homie. Be safe young blood." B-Mo finally said, and started to serve a lick that had just walked up for his dose.

"Yo Trip come by later to my crib and I got you. Said Damion.

"Damn damu, I got people waiting on me." Protested Trip.

"Shit man. Here take this. I'll holler at you later. Now go!" Damion put all the rocks in Trips hand. He wanted him gone from there. Now.

"Alright Blood. Peace," said Trip and turned to leave.

Everything was silent for a minute before B-Mo said anything.

"That pistol is exactly the same type they say that killed Re-Re." B-Mo said.

"Small world." Damion just said.

"I was thinking the exact same thing when I was holding his gun. It felt weird Damion. I can't explain it dawg." B-Mo said looking ahead.

"Man dawg you're over thinking things. That pistol probably across the border with them Mexicans." Damion said trying to evade coincidence.

"Yeah you're probably right. If that crab motherfucker is smart he wouldn't keep that pistol. I wouldn't." B-Mo said.

"Right. Come on dawg. Let me buy you a forty and then I'm bouncing. I got shit to do." Damion said changing the subject.

"You mean do someone." B-Mo said laughing. He knew his homie. At least he thought he did.

"Friend or Foe" By: DJ Screw.

143

Chapter 35

After we left Randy's crib me and Ro decided it was a good idea to go see our boy Rico again and get a few things off of him. My boy was really plugged in. Big time! If you needed something he was the guy to see. He ain't failed me yet.

"Babe! What club we going to?" Asked Reneé while she sat at her vanity doing her makeup.

"Metropolis!" I told her ironing my slacks and button down Ralph Lauren shirt I got at the mall earlier. I had to get a fade and some clothes for tonight. I needed to unwind 'cause of all the stress I had and plus Reneé wanted two go out anyway.

I called Kevin and got the address I needed to make sure everything was still on. So far so good. 30 minutes later Ro was outside honking. Me and baby stepped out the house and we looked and smelled like a million bucks together. Reneé had on a royal blue minidress with high heels complimenting her legs and made her ass pop even more. Hair straight and makeup on point. Baby made me proud and made me look good with my royal blue shirt creased up as well as my pants with dress shoes.

I sprayed some Burberry classic Cologne on it. I had to pull Reneé off of me twice. Had to save that for later. It was going down! It was 12:45 and the club was still bumbing and jumping, and the line was still long with people trying to get in. Ro got the ride detailed while we shopped and its tires were still wet when we pulled up to VIP parking. Ro didn't have a date, my nigga had it on his mind to leave with a broad or two at the end of the night.

Ro called Rico earlier as well to let him know we were going to be pulling up. Sometimes it's not what you know, but who you know. Ro gave the bouncer a $20 and told him who we were and that our party was waiting on us. The bouncer nodded his head and opened the chain post for us and we strutted in.

They was playing some bachata and Reneé started dancing walking beside me and my hand went to her ass cheek. The material of her dress felt so thin, almost like skin and I knew a secret that I just found out myself in the back seat of Ro's ride on our way up here. Couldn't keep my hands to myself, what can I say?

We headed straight to the VIP section and once Rico saw us he jumped to his feet and beckoned for us to come up to where he was with a bunch of hoes and a few niggas.

"You can only look baby, but if you behave you might be able to touch." Reneé said. Did I mention that Reneé had a girlfriend one time? No? My fault.

"Oye, que lo que es!?" Hollered Rico over the loud music.

"What's good bro?!" I hollered back.

"Oyé pues quien es esta bellesa?" Rico asked, referring to Rneé and kissed her on the hand.

This my girl Reneé . Babe, this my boy Rico." I introduced them.

"Hi." Said Reneé nervously.

145

"What ya'll drinking? It's on me!" Rico said and called a waitress over to us.

"Whatever you got bro." I tell Rico. Ro said wassup and went straight for the hoes and did his thing.

Rico got us both a drink and hugged me after that. "You good bro?" He asked me.

"Yeah, yeah. I'ma need some shit off you. I got something coming up." I said over the loud music.

Esta bien. We'll talk later. You think about what I asked you?" He told me.

"Yeah. I'll do it, but let me take care of this others shit first." I said. "

OK. But don't take too long. I need this done by next week." He tells me and I just nod. I can see Reneé bouncing in her seat and it made her titties jiggle. Rico noticed it too and smiled.

"Sacala' a bailar cabrón! We'll meet tomorrow afternoon. Have fun!" He told me, hugged me and takes off to where Ro was and starts to chop it up with him and the fine bitches around there.

"Want to dance baby?" I say to Reneé putting my hand out for her to take.

"About time papi, I thought you'd never ask." She replied eager to hit the dance floor.

Reneé takes my hand and gets up. I smack her on the ass as she walks ahead of me and we head to the dance floor. Nicky Jam is doing his shit and got hoes bouncing their ass everywhere! Reneé spins in front of me and we start to grinding to the reggaeton music and her ass is rubbing on my dick up and down. I got busy right behind her and did my damn thing. Like that black guy said on the movie "Happy Gilmore" "It's all in the hips."

Chapter 36

<u>Thursday Morning.</u>

B-Mo was standing in front of Damion. He had an evil sinister look in his eyes and then his hand came up into Damion's view. The pistol was covered in blood, red like the color of clothes that B-Mo was wearing only darker.

"You did it dawg. You killed Re Re!" B-Mo said loudly.

"No! It was an accident. I didn't mean to!" Pleaded Damion.

"You killed her and now I'm going to kill you, Blood." B-Mo snarled and then the gun went off.

(Pow)

"No!' Damion screamed and jumped out of bed breathing hard and sweating.

"Baby what's wrong?" Said the voice next to him and it startled Damion. It was just a bad dream he thought a started to relax.

"Yeah, yeah I'm good. Just had a dream that I was falling." He lied.

"Oh yeah, I've had that dream before too." She said and laughed.

She got close to him and put a hand on his thigh while her bare tits rubbed his arm. "Want me to make that bad dream turn into a wet dream?" She said with a giggle.

"I'd love that but I got to go ma. Some other time." He says and gets out of bed to get dressed.

Melissa did the same and went to her closet and draped a t-shirt on her that belonged to her husband that was locked up. Damion couldn't figure out why the chicks he fucked with were Mexican, with a man locked up and a gang of kids? But hey somebody had to take care of these hoes out here.. Poor suckers thought 'cause they was locked up that their girls were going to keep the pussy on lock. Yeah right! Women got needs and phone sex just doesn't cut it.

That's why Damion didn't keep a chick as his girl, 'cause like Chris Brown said. "These hoes ain't loyal."

Damion's cell vibrated. Somebody was calling. It was B-Mo.

"What's poppin'?" Damion answered. He listened and then responded "Alright, when?" Damion asked. "On my way. Peace." Damion said and hung up.

"Everything okay papi?" Asked Melissa.

"Yeah, I got to go ma." He said and peeled a couple of bills. Always support the hustle.

"Mmm papi. You sure you don't want to stay? I'll make you some breakfast in bed." She said wrapping her arms around Damion.

"Nah ma, I'd love to stay but I got to go." He said and headed out and He was almost to the door when suddenly he heard the noise.

"Pow, pow!" Screamed the little boy with a toy gun in his hand and pointing it at Damion. It scared the shit out of Damion so bad that he tripped but caught himself against the wall.

"What the fuck?" Said Damion in surprise.

"Frankie! No! Bad boy! Melissa said chastising her son.

"Sorry." She then told Damion.

"It's cool. He just surprised me." Damion said, grabbed the door knob and left.

Once the door closed behind him Melissa grabbed Little Frankie that was only four by the hand. "Frankie don't be that way with the electrician. It's the plumber that plays pow, pow with you." She told him and carried him to the kitchen. "You want pa pa's. You hungry?" Melissa asked her baby.

"Late night tip"

By: Three Six Mafia

Damion made it back to his hood from Spring Ranch in 15 minutes and was cursing the whole way.

He was mad at himself 'cause he knew what he was supposed to have done, but didn't. Now it was going two bite him in the ass. No wonder he had that dream he had. He pulls up to B-Mo's complex and jumps out and power walks into the trap house.

"Christine! Bitch is nasty, but that ass is clean!" One of the 'ol heads said after he slammed a domino on the table. "Give me my money nigga!" He ordered.

"Yo, where B-Mo at?" Damion asked.

"Inside." Another OG said pointing.

Damion goes in and sees B-Mo chillin on the couch and a thick yellow boned bitch damn near naked next to him as they smoked a blunt.

"Wassup?" Damion came in and sat down on the sofa chair.

"Trips. mom came by a lil while ago to tell me that he got jammed up by the laws last night serving a fiend at the corner store." B-Mo said high as a kite.

Must've been right after we saw him. Said Damion sitting down.

"I had some shit to do so I didn't see him after that." Damion continued.

"So what they get him for?" Asked Damion when B-Mo didn't say anything.

"Dope charge. Selling to an undercover." B-Mo said and blew smoke out.

Damion leaned back in his sofa and relaxed.

"Oh yeah, and he got caught with that nice pistol he had." B-Mo added.

Damion tensed and B-Mo noticed it. He was looking for a reaction.

"I told his mom to let me know as soon as she hears anything and I gave her a few bills to put on the homies books. B-Mo said matter of factly.

"Yeah I'll get some bread together and see about helping him get a lawyer. Damion said.

"Fasho." B-Mo said and continued to smoke.

"Alright. I got shit to do dawg. Hit me up later." Damion said and got up to go.

"I bet." B-Mo said and looked at Damion. "Come on Teetee. I got something to holla at you about." B-Mo tells the girl next to him and smacks her on the ass as she walked to the room to talk.

By the time Damion made it to the jail for juveniles it was past lunch so the streets weren't as crowded in downtown. He paid for parking, got out and went into the jail. Filled out the visitation slip and gave the cop the slip and his ID when he was up next in line.

"Third floor." Said the cop and stamped the slip and gave it back but kept the ID.

Damion goes up the elevator to the third floor. He takes the slip to the window and drops it in the metal slot that is retracted by another cop.

"Booth 18" The cop said on the intercom and Damion goes in and waited.

About 15 minutes later Trip is escorted to where Damion is and sits down. Damion picks up the black phone and indicates for Trip to do the same. He did. "What's up homie?" How you holding up? Damion asked.

Trip looks sick and sad and like he's been crying.

"You alright? They feeding you?" Damion asked sounding really concerned.

Trip just nodded his head.

"So what happened?" Damion pressed.

"After I left you and B-Mo I went back to the store and a white lady came up to me dressed like a dope fiend, so I served her and then the laws ran down on me." Trip explained speaking low.

"Then what?" Asked Damion trying to get as much info as possible.

"They put cuffs on me and then searched me." Trip said.

"And what they find on you?" Asked Damion and got serious.

"My money, some rocks and the gun." Trip said and put his head down. Now his true age showed Damion noticed.

"So what you tell them when they asked about the gun?" Asked Damion pressing on.

"I told them I bought it off a dope fiend like you told me." Said Trip looking up.

"Good. That's good bro. You did good." Damion said, relieved.

"Look, you're going to be okay. We're going to help you get a lawyer, so if they try to ask you anything else just tell them you want a lawyer." Damion instructed Trip.

Trip just nodded and it looked like he felt better now.

"Just keep yo head up and don't take shit from anybody lil homie. " You're a Blood so rep that shit to the fullest." Damion told Trip and brought color back to his face. Now the lil homie looked back to normal.

"I'ma put some money on your books and if you need anything tell your mom and tell her to come to me. Nobody else. I got you. You my lil homie. Aight?" Damion said sternly.

Trip nodded and looked better now.

"Keep quiet and don't say shit. You'll be alright, I promise damu." Damion said and put his fist on the glass and Trip did the same. "

Real or Fake"

By: Z-Ro ft. Chris Ward

Chapter 37

8:57PM

Me and Ro made it to north side with no problem. I texted Kevin twice on the way just to make sure it was still a go 'cause once we got to that point of no return it was over with. We parked the Astro van a few houses from the guys place, but could still have a really good view. Everything was quiet and peaceful at the moment so we was good and started getting ready. All we needed. was for him to pull up from the date he was on, wait a bit and go in. Until then we waited.

"Here." Ro said passing me a bullet proof vest.

"Mayne hold up!" I said excited. "Big Rico really came through huh?

"Hell yeah." Ro said with a grin.

We picked up the vests from Rico earlier today, and we both got some new toys! Ro got a .45 and I got me a 9mm Barretta., nickel plated with black handle covers. I fell in love with it as soon as Rico showed it to me. All in all I paid $550 total. Not bad.

The van was free. Somebody will miss it in the morning. It worked great and the a/c worked. Plus it had a CD player and I had popped in one of my own so we could jam out. Three Six Mafia was rapping us into existence. We really didn't have a plan 'cause we both know that plans tend to suck and not work out how you expect them to.

We knew what had to be done and what we were after, point blank period.

The van was super foggy from us smoking when there was a really nice Chevy truck pulling up into the house driveway an hour and a half later.

"Here we go." I said to Ro sitting up in my seat.

We saw the couple exit and go inside. It was dark but the two figures were unmistakable. One man and one woman. So far so good. After they went in I waited about ten minutes and spoke.

"I'll be back Ro." I said.

"Where you going nigga?" Asked Ro.

"To look around and make sure ain't no bullshit gonna get in our way and peep the scene. Chill, I'll be back. Be ready." I say getting out and closing the door as quietly as possible.

My all black Polo boots didn't make a sound as I crept up to the side of the house and stopped and listened. No barking. Good. I go to the gate , open it softly by the hatch and creep around slowly to the window in the back. I heard music playing and recognized Marco Antonio Solis' voice instantly. A well known singer in the Latino community and when I tell you that this dude is the reason why Hispanics multiplied so much you'd think I was bullshitting. Shit I probably was conceived 'cause of him and his vocal cords.

All of a sudden I heard a bed squeaking and a woman's moan in pleasure escaped the window. They were in the middle of something.

Perfect. I ran back to get Ro but still cautious. Our window of opportunity was now.

I got to the door and opened the door with my gloved hand.

"Let's go nigga. Now or never!" I tell Ro and grab my ski mask and put it on.

Ro slid his over his head and cocks his gun and gets out. Showtime!

We didn't hesitate and get straight to business. Ro was first and kicked the door in with all his weight and I was right behind him. My flashlight came on and lit the way and we just followed the music to the room I shined my light on his naked ass pounding away and that got his attention.

"Que chingaos?!" The mustache man said mad coming off 'ol girl.

"Shut the fuck up!" Ro said and pistol whipped the dude. It happened so fast. The lady began to scream.

"Shut up bitch! Scream again and I'll kill you." I said to a blanket covered figure, she had covered herself real fast. She didn't scream anymore but I could hear her whimper.

Ol' boy was holding his hand on his head where Ro hit him. I finally turn the room light on. It made him use his other arm to put over his face 'cause of the sudden brightness. Ro kicked the side of the bed and the woman whimpered again.

"Where's the money?" I ask calmly.

"Money? Jwat Money?" He said in pain and in wet back English.

"Oh, so you want to play games pendejo!?" I tell him.

Ro punched the guy.

"Ayi. OK, OK. Espera! Jwait!" He pleaded with palms out.

That got his heart right real quick.

"Ju want money? In there!" He said, pointing to a closet.

"Say ma, come up from under the blanket." I tell the crying figure.

I could hear her whimpering and sniffling. The total opposite sounds she was making before we so rudely interrupted the party. She didn't do as I said the first time and I wasn't going to ask again. I grabbed the blanket, pull it off of her toss it to the side and freeze in place 'cause of what I was looking at. Actually at who I was looking at, it blew my mind.

"Come on nigga. We ain't got time for a peep show. Go to the closet!" Ro said and snapped me back to the mission at hand.

"Don't shoot me please. I beg you." My aunt Lilly said crying and pleading naked.

I picked a shirt off the floor and toss it to her. I didn't want to talk anymore afraid she'll recognize my voice. I could feel Ro looking at me like "What the fuck?" as I went to the safe.

"Locked!" I said as little as possible .

"Oye' pendejo. What's the code?' Barked Ro to the man but got no response.

(Whack!)

He started rattling off numbers in Spanish so fast. That iron is square business. I punched in the code and it opens on the first try. I see a lot of cash and jewelry and stuff every bit of it into my canvas bag leaving the safe empty.

I got up to go and. I gestured with my head to Ro I got it and then to go. No words needed.

"If you move I'll kill you. You hear me?" Ro warned and we both ran out of there. Ro grabs the dudes keys off the table by the door and barely made it out the front door when a gun goes off disturbing the quiet of the night.

(BAM!)

I duck instantly, but Ro hits his knee beside me on the yard. That's when I turned around and saw a figure coming.

"Pinches putos! Hijos de sus chigada madres!" He yelled and was about to fire again when I let off two shots his way and he was still able to take a shot my way but went somewhere else. He gained his balance again to shoot when I realized he wasn't going to stop. So I let him have it.

(Pop, pop, pop, pop, pop)

I emptied my clip and that's when I realized he'd fallen within the first few shots. I feel Ro's hand push against me and see he's trying to give me the keys and trying to get up. It was a lot closer than the van. So I grabbed Ro and picked him up. By this time neighbors start to turn on their porch lights so I knew we had to go. Now!

I put him in the back seat and jump behind the wheel of the truck that was jacked up a bit. Turned it on and it roared to life. I put that bitch in reverse, came out the driveway and put it in drive once I got it straight on the street. The V8 350/engine had some giddy up 'cause I burned rubber out of there.

Once I got to the main street I slowed down.

"Where you hit Ro?" I ask looking back at my boy.

"My leg." He said and winced.

"Alright hold on cuzz. Let's get you to Freddie's crib." I said.

Freddie is another one of our homies, his girl is an RN for Memorial hospital. She'll know what to do. I got on 45 and headed south and I was hauling ass! I kept checking on my boy Ro making sure he was still conscious and ain't passed out on me, or worse die.

But I couldn't stop thinking about what just happened. I couldn't believe I bumped into my aunt Lilly like that What the fuck was she doing there. I knew what she was doing, duh. But God damn why him? Why tonight? And to top it all off I had just killed a man!

I didn't feel too bad 'cause to be honest Ro did warn him and he did shoot at us first. So it was justifiable then. Right?

"Stay with me Ro!" I yelled to him.

"I'm good bro, just drive." Ro said calmly. So I drove, and was about to turn the radio on when it dawned on me. My CD was still in the running Astro van parked a few houses down from where I just killed a guy.

"Oh Shit!" I yelled.

Aimless Triggers—Jose C. Hernandez Jr.

Great, just great.

"Game Untold"

By: South Park Mexican

To Be Continued....

www.ingramcontent.com/pod-product-compliance
Lightning Source LLC
Chambersburg PA
CBHW070655100726
47907CB00007B/2217